FLYING SOLO

By Ralph Fletcher

HOUGHTON MIFFLIN HARCOURT
BOSTON • NEW YORK

For information about permission to reproduce selections from this book,
write to trade.permissions @ hmhco.com or to Permissions, Houghton Mifflin
Harcourt Publishing Company, 3 Park Avenue, 19th Floor, New York, New York
10016

www.hmhco.com

The text was set in 12/15 Walbaum.

Library of Congress Cataloging-in-Publication Data

Fletcher, Ralph.
Flying solo / Ralph Fletcher.
p.   cm.
Summary: Rachel, having chosen to be mute following the
sudden death of a classmate, shares responsibility with the
other sixth-graders who decide not to report that the substitute
teacher failed to show up.
HC ISBN-13: 978-0-395-87323-6
PA ISBN-13: 978-0-547-07652-2
[1. Schools — Fiction. 2. Teachers — Fiction. 3. Mutism,
Elective — Fiction. 4. Death — Fiction.] I. Title.
PZ7.F632115F1 1998
[Fic] — dc21   98-10775
CIP
AC

Printed in the United States of America
DOC 20 19 18 17 16
4500762578

For my boys—Joseph, Robert, Adam, and Taylor

Friday, April 28

7:03 A.M.

—— Rachel White ——

Rachel lay in bed, reading, waiting until the last possible minute when she absolutely had to put down her book and get out of bed.

Many people believe that it is the air passing under the wings that supports the plane as it flies, she read. *In fact, it is the air passing* over *the wings that provides the lift that keeps the airplane in the air.*

"Rachel!" Mom yelled. "C'mon, gal, shake a leg!"

Rachel sighed and looked up from her book at the posters around her bedroom. Amelia Earhart. Charles Lindbergh. Sally Ride. John Glenn. It was hard to believe that they all had to go to school, too.

Rachel swung her legs out of bed and stumbled into the bathroom. She didn't look forward to school much these last six months. There wasn't much to enjoy, except for Mr. Fabiano.

He was by far the greatest teacher she had ever had. Smart and funny. And simply gorgeous, with black-black eyes that could always find a place deep inside her. She had a crush on him, all right, not that she was alone. Most of the other sixth-grade girls had crushes on "Mr. Fab."

She would never call him that nickname. No way. It made her think of Fab laundry detergent. She would always think of him as Mr. Fabiano.

Rachel leaned forward to wash her face with cold water. She brushed her teeth, rinsed her mouth, and cleared her throat.

The guttural sound startled her. There was a hint of her voice in that sound and she had not heard her voice in the past six months.

She remembered the day it happened. Tommy Feathers, a kid in her sixth-grade class, had brought to class some raspberry pies he'd made at his parents' bakery. Tommy had brought a wedge of pie for everyone, but he put the biggest piece of pie on her desk.

Tommy smiled at her. He had a rather big head, and an annoying habit of humming loudly in class. He was a little slow—already he had been kept back twice, so he was two years older than anybody else in sixth grade. It was no secret that he was in love with her. Every day he tried to give her cards, stories, seashells, and now this huge chunk of raspberry pie. She tried not to be mean, but sometimes he really got on her nerves.

"I don't like sweets," she said, pushing the pie back toward him.

After school Tommy showed up at her house, something he had never done before.

"I made you a whole pie," he said, grinning and holding it out to her. "A whole pie made from yellow raspberries. They're like gold. Gold is my favorite color."

"Golden raspberries?" Mom exclaimed. "Really? How marvelous! I never heard of such a thing."

"We picked them in New Hampshire," Tommy explained, still flashing that foolish grin. "In New Hampshire."

"I told you I don't like pie," Rachel told Tommy. "I don't eat sweets. How many times do I have to tell you?"

Tommy lowered his eyes and bit his lower lip.

"Well, I certainly do," Mom said, taking the pie from him. "Thank you, Tommy. I'm going to enjoy every bite."

That was on October 28. Next morning her best friend Missy phoned to tell her the news. Tommy Feathers was dead.

"He died in his sleep," Missy said.

"Oh my God," Rachel whispered into the telephone.

She stared at the TV, a stupid cop show. A detective had just handcuffed a suspect, and the man looked guilty: scruffy beard, haunted eyes,

3

wild hair. The detective started to read the man his rights.

"You have the right to remain silent," he began.

"What does *that* mean?" the suspect interrupted.

"It means you have the right to be quiet," the detective snapped. "Now shut up and listen."

Rachel was half-aware of Missy's voice in her ear, talking over the telephone, but she couldn't get beyond those five words. *The right to remain silent.* She could see them in her head:

The   right   to   remain   silent.

"What happened?" Mom asked when Rachel put down the phone, and Rachel tried to answer. She tried to say it—*Tommy Feathers is dead*—she reached deep down inside herself to find those words, but they were cold when she touched them. Frozen. She knew those words could never fly.

Things got pretty crazy after that. Mom talked to her. Pleaded. Begged. Cried. That night, and for many nights after, Mom held Rachel in her arms. Mom wept and talked and begged some more.

"Why won't you talk to your mother?" Mom asked.

"I can't," Rachel wrote on a small pad of paper.

Oh my God. Her last word: *God.*

Her father telephoned all the way from his cattle ranch in New Mexico. Rachel held the phone against her cheek and tried to picture him, the hat and expensive boots, while she listened to his voice.

"I don't get it," he said. "A boy in your class dies and you stop talking. It makes no sense. What's the connection?"

Rachel breathed into the phone.

Mom set up appointments with counselors, psychologists, therapists. A specialist named Dr. Bang-Jansen diagnosed her as a *selective mute:* a person who chooses not to speak. She explained to Rachel and her mother that often this kind of reaction is caused by some kind of profound emotional trauma.

"The condition is temporary," Dr. Bang-Jansen said. "Usually."

Sometimes Mom wrote notes, too. They'd make a pot of tea and sit at the kitchen table, both of them silent, writing back and forth.

I'm so worried about you.

I'm okay, Mom.

Your father said it is as if your voice died along with that poor boy. I told him: Her voice isn't dead—it's only sleeping.

Maybe.

Or maybe it's just frozen. There must be some way to thaw it out.

Writing notes back and forth helped to reas-

sure Mom a tiny bit. But now there was a pan-
icky light in her eyes.

The doorbell rang. It was Missy, come to walk
her to school.

"Hi, Missy," Mom said.

"Hi, Mrs. White," Missy said.

Mom turned back to look at Rachel.

"You look terrific," she said. "You always look
smashing in that skirt."

Rachel leaned into Mom's hug.

"Keep your eyes peeled on the way to school,"
Mom whispered. "Okay, honey? And if you happen to spot that voice of yours lying on the
ground, well, just pick it up and bring it home."

Rachel closed her eyes and nodded. Mom said
the same thing, word for word, every morning.

7:05 A.M.

———— Bastian Fauvell ————

The instant Bastian opened his eyes he saw Barkley, curled up at the edge of his bed, staring up with eyes the color of gold coins.

"C'mon, boy!" he whispered. Barkley bounded forward and began eagerly licking his face.

"Hey, take it easy!" Bastian looked down at the puppy. Part German shepherd and part retriever, Barkley had fur and eyes the same golden color.

"You're going on a big trip today," he told the puppy. "You won't see me for a couple days. But you'll be okay. Really. You'll do great. Here, go get it!"

He took a little Nerf football and threw it. This sent the puppy scampering madly across the room. Barkley grabbed the football and brought it back to Bastian.

"C'mon, Bastian!" Mom yelled. "You don't want to be late! It's your last day of school!"

"Good boy!" Bastian said, taking the football.

7

He got out of bed. *Last day of school.* He repeated it over and over. By now moving was no big deal. He had moved before and he'd move again. For Air Force brats that's how it would always be. Twelve years old and this would be his eighth move. He could rattle off the eight different bases for anyone who cared to listen:

1) Kadena Air Force Base in Okinawa
2) Langley Air Force Base in Virginia
3) Nellis Air Force Base in Nevada
4) Eglin Air Force Base in Florida
5) Luke Air Force Base in Arizona
6) Maxwell Air Force Base in Alabama
7) Seymour Johnson Air Force Base in North Carolina
8) Shaw Air Force Base in South Carolina

He couldn't remember Okinawa—he'd been just a baby then—but he could remember all the other places, every military base or town, every cramped apartment and officers' barracks, the PXs and commissaries. And all his best friends: Chad, Drew, Troy, Connor, John. Their pictures were taped into his scrapbook.

Now his father was being transferred to Hickham Air Force Base in Honolulu, Hawaii. Bastian didn't mind that. Hawaii was a place he'd always wanted to see. Moving again would be a cinch if it wasn't for Barkley. And the Quarantine.

When Dad first explained about the Quarantine, Bastian couldn't believe it. The military authorities wanted to prevent contagious germs from contaminating Hawaiian animals. They were worried that any animal coming into Hawaii might have a disease it could give to other animals. That's why they had the Quarantine. They had strict rules: Any dog coming into Hawaii had to be quarantined, kept away by itself, until they were sure the dog didn't have any contagious disease. Barkley would be quarantined for four months.

That's crazy! Barkley doesn't have any disease! he told his dad.

I know. But the military makes the rules, and we have to follow them. They can't take any chances. There's no exceptions.

Well, that's the stupidest rule I've ever heard!

I know it will be hard on you, Dad said. *But it's going to be even harder on Barkley. Do you really want to put a puppy through all that? It's something to think about, Bastian. I know you love him, but maybe you should consider leaving Barkley here.*

Leave him here? Are you kidding?

I'm sure we could find a family who could take care of him.

No way! I want my dog.

All right, then.

Can't I visit him when he's quarantined?

Yes. But I'm warning you: It's still going to be hard.

In the kitchen his mother was standing on a stepladder, taking plates from a cabinet. There were boxes everywhere.

"Got anything to eat, Ma?"

"There's cereal," she said. "Shredded wheat."

"Shredded wheat," he groaned. "Why don't they just call it shredded newspaper? That's how it tastes."

"This isn't a restaurant," she retorted. "And I can't stop to fix you anything else because I've got to pack this kitchen."

Whistling, Dad walked into the kitchen. He was wearing a crisply ironed uniform, hair neatly combed and gleaming.

"Is your room all packed?" he asked.

"No."

"You need to do that first thing after school," he said. "We've got to be completely packed tonight. We're leaving tomorrow morning at 0-dark-thirty."

"Okay." Bastian poured a bowl of shredded wheat. Barkley sat on the floor watching Bastian shovel the cereal into his mouth. The Nerf football was resting between the puppy's paws.

"What time does Barkley's flight leave tonight?" he asked Dad.

"Six o'clock sharp," he said.

"I'm coming to the airport," Bastian said, picking Barkley up. "You'll get to Hawaii first, you lucky dog."

At the airport they would give Barkley a shot to make him sleep for the long flight to Hawaii. Bastian pictured the puppy, scared and alone on the plane. Then the Quarantine. Four months. A hundred and twenty-two days of solitary confinement in a cage. Or maybe there would be other dogs. He didn't know.

"I'm gonna visit you every day," Bastian promised. "And twice on Saturdays. Okay?"

Barkley looked up hopefully. The phone rang.

"Yo, Bastian?" It was John LeClerc, his best friend at school.

"Hey. What's up?"

"Not much," John said. "I'm staying home today. Very bad stomachache. I was thinking you might have one, too. Do you?"

"I can't," Bastian said, grinning. "It's my last day."

"I thought your last day was Monday."

"Dad changed his mind. We're leaving tomorrow. I gotta pack my stuff right after school."

"Okay, it's your funeral," John said. "Just don't blame me if you die of boredom today."

"Yeah, yeah, yeah."

"Hey, I guess I won't see you before you move. Have a nice life."

Bastian threw Barkley the Nerf football, and the dog caught it in his mouth. The puppy looked up, eyes full of golden light and perfect trust.

"Yeah, you too."

7:08 A.M.

——Jessica Cooke——

She stared at herself in the bathroom mirror. Amazing how skinny she had grown. And tall. She was the tallest kid in the whole sixth grade. Which suited her fine. Jessica didn't mind being different.

"Breakfast!" Mom called.

"Okay!" Jessica yelled. She gave her hair three more brushes—forty-eight, forty-nine, fifty—wheeled out of the bathroom, and ran down to the kitchen. Monica, Jessica's three-year-old sister, was sitting on the floor. "Hi, Monica. Hi, Mom. Boy, am I hungry."

"You could use some meat on your bones," Mom said. "You want a waffle? Scrambled eggs? Fruit salad? Cereal?"

"All of the above," Jessica replied, nodding. "I'm starving."

"Morning, ladies!" Dad said, walking into the kitchen. He poured himself a cup of coffee and sat down at the table.

"Hi, Dad. Nice suit."

12

"Thanks," he said, smiling at her. "What's going on in school, Jessica? How's Mr. Fabiano?"

"Mr. Fab is fabulous." She poured herself a large bowl of cereal. "Next week we're going to start a research project."

"On . . . ?"

"My Future Profession," Jessica said. "Like, what we want to be when we grow up."

"And you want to be a lawyer, right?" He smiled at her. "Like father, like daughter."

"Nope," she said. "I want to be the chief justice of the Supreme Court."

"Nice," he said, nodding. "But most Supreme Court justices are judges first. And most judges are lawyers first."

"You'd make a fine lawyer," Mom said, putting a plate of scrambled eggs in front of her. "You've got the mind for it."

"Yes, and the law is important," Dad said. "Without the law there would be total anarchy."

Monica ran over and took the seat next to Jessica.

"What are you going to be when you grow up?" Jessica asked her.

"A horsey rider," Monica said, dead serious. "Can you teach me? Please?"

"I've got to go to school," Jessica told her.

"I thought today was a home day," Monica said sadly.

"Nope, it's Friday. Tomorrow's a home day."

13

"Here's your waffle," Mom said to Monica.

"Let me help you cut it," Jessica offered.

"No, I do it mySELF!" Monica said. She stabbed her fork into the waffle, but it slid off the plate and knocked over her cup. Orange juice spilled onto the table and all over Dad's suit.

"She can't do it herself!" Dad yelled, jumping up. "What were you thinking? For heaven's sake, she's only three years old!"

"Sorry, Dad," Jessica said.

"Now I've got to go change!" Dad stormed out of the kitchen.

—— Sean O'Day ——

He was walking with a dog. They were walking through a huge mansion with many large and beautiful rooms, but the house was the forest and the rooms were made by trees. The trunks grew close together to form walls, and he found he could walk through the walls and enter clearings lit from above by soft light that flickered as it sifted through the leafy branches. He entered one forest room where the light was so green and pure he sat down for a moment and closed his eyes. The dog came and sat close by him. It was quiet. He sat with his hunting rifle, holding it loosely with the safety on and the chamber empty.

"Hey!"

A hand roughly shook his shoulder.

"Hey, wake up!"

Sean blinked open his eyes and saw Darlene. He groaned and rubbed his eyes. He hated getting bumped out of a dream, especially a sweet dream like that.

"C'mon, Bud. It's almost quarter past! You better get a move on or you'll miss the bus."

He glanced at the clock—barely twenty minutes before the school bus came. He waited until Darlene left the room before he got out of bed. From the top drawer he dug out a clean pair of socks but he couldn't find any clean T-shirts. And not a single pair of clean underwear, either. He went to the pile of clothes on the floor and dug through them until he found a pair of shorts and a T-shirt that didn't look too bad.

In the kitchen Darlene was sipping a cup of coffee and staring out the window. Behind her, on the counter, Sean made a quick count of the empty green beer bottles. Eleven.

"Top of the morning to you," she said.

"Hi." He didn't have to ask where Dad was. Passed out in the bedroom. Sleeping it off.

"You've got quite a pile of dirty clothes in your room," Darlene said. "Smells like a locker room in there. Would you do me a favor, Sean? Pick up those clothes and throw them into the washing machine? I'll run it through."

"Yeah, okay. I'll do it after school."

Darlene sometimes reminded Sean of Dad's last girlfriend, Carla. Carla had been ten years younger than Dad, and Darlene was even younger than that. She was twenty-two, barely ten years older than Sean.

He opened the fridge.

"We got any bagels?" he asked.

"We're out," Darlene said. "I'll get some when I go shopping today. You want some scrambled eggs?"

"No."

"Well, you better eat something," she said.

"Don't got time," he answered, even though his stomach was growling something fierce. He yanked a can of soda from a six-pack and tucked it into his knapsack. Then he went back to his room, grabbed a candy bar from the top of his bureau, and slipped out of the house.

7:19 A.M.

—— Mrs. Muchmore ——

Wendy Muchmore woke with a throbbing headache. Every bone in her body ached; every joint was on fire. She wanted to go back to sleep, but she couldn't. Today she was subbing in Mr. Fabiano's sixth-grade class at the Paulson Elementary School. She had to be there by 8:12 A.M. sharp.

She tried to sit up, but lifting her head brought on such a fit of dizziness she felt like throwing up. She groaned. There was no choice but to call in and take a sick day. They would have to find a substitute for the substitute. With some effort, she lifted the heavy phone book and found the number of the school.

"Paulson Elementary School."

"Yes, good morning, this is Mrs. Muchmore." Her voice sounded shaky. "I'm scheduled to substitute for Mr. Fabiano today, sixth grade. Unfor-

18

tunately I'm sick today so I can't come in. I'm so—"

"You're supposed to call the Registry when you're sick." It was Mrs. Pierce, the school secretary, and she sounded annoyed. "That's district policy. Didn't they tell you that?"

"Yes, well, I forgot—"

"I'll make a note of it," Mrs. Pierce said, "but next time please phone the Registry." She hung up. Wendy sighed and put down the phone.

7:56 A.M.

— The Principal's Office —

Irwin Peacock sat in his office listening to Peggy Ransom. He had the door closed and a rubber band wrapped tight around his thumbs. Peggy was the mother of a student, Christopher, in Mr. Fabiano's sixth-grade class. More important, she was president of the P.T.A.

"I'll tell you this—a lot of parents in this district are concerned about that sixth-grade team of yours," Mrs. Ransom said. "Deeply concerned. Pat Kiefer is one teacher who never should have been hired. Sally Walker is in that class, her mother is a close friend of mine, and according to her, Pat Kiefer does not teach. Every day after school she asks Sally 'What did you learn today?' and Sally just stares at her. Learned? Huh?"

Mr. Peacock leaned forward and rubbed his temples. As a principal he listened to lots of difficult parents, but there was nobody worse than

20

Peggy Ransom. He dreaded his weekly chats with this woman with her Jaguar, her five-hundred-dollar leather jackets, the rings that sported enormous diamonds on both hands.

He closed his eyes. Ninety-eight percent of the parents in the district were wonderful, but the other two percent made him wish he worked as a farmer. Or a forest ranger.

"Dana Friedman is supposed to be your superstar, but she's gone to conferences half the time," Mrs. Ransom was saying. "I mean, what good is she if she's always out of the classroom? Myrna Reilly has her kids brainwashed into following every liberal cause she can get her hands on. And then you've got that cutie pie, Sal Fabiano. There's something very strange going on in that class. As far as I can see, he doesn't do any skill work at all. Kids like him, sure, because he doesn't make them work. What's not to like? From what my son tells me, all the kids do is read and write. What ever happened to teaching spelling? Or grammar?"

Irwin Peacock tried to make it look as if he were listening hard. The woman's voice was about as pleasant as a chainsaw—he could feel it cutting into him.

"Okay, Peggy, I hear you," Mr. Peacock said, breaking the rubber band wrapped around his thumbs. "But my hands are tied. There's no way I can make any changes in that sixth-grade team. Especially not now at the end of the year. You must—"

"I think it's disgraceful!" Peggy Ransom said, storming out of his office. She swept past Mrs. Pierce's desk and knocked a stack of phone messages onto the floor. One of the phone messages fell against the radiator where it got caught, out of sight.

"I've got a good mind to pull my son out of this place and put him into a decent private school," Peggy said loudly. "Where teachers understand the three Rs and aren't afraid to teach them!"

Mr. Peacock called after her: "I hope you don't, but you do have that right." And thinking: *I should only be so lucky.*

First Bell

Rachel stood with Missy on the playground. At exactly 8:10 A.M. she gave Missy a see-ya-in-a-minute look and slipped in through the door. She had almost reached her classroom when the first bell rang.

Rachel loved coming to class early because it gave her a few quiet moments alone with Mr. Fabiano. He would stand by her desk talking to her, never pressuring her to talk back, and it was a pleasure simply to be near him and feel his words wash over her. Now she entered Room 238 and looked around, but the room was empty. *Where was Mr. Fabiano?* Rachel wondered. Then she spied the large block letters on the blackboard:

CLASS 6-238,
    GOOD MORNING! YOU WILL HAVE A
SUBSTITUTE TEACHER TODAY. I KNOW

23

YOU WILL GIVE TO MRS. MUCHMORE THE
SAME RESPECT AND ATTENTION YOU
WOULD GIVE TO ME. YOU ALL KNOW THE
ROUTINE FOR FRIDAY. SEE YOU ON MON-
DAY.

MR. FABIANO

Rachel stamped her foot and the sharp sound echoed in the deserted classroom. Substitute! As if anyone could substitute for Mr. Fabiano. It was the worst, most depressing way to start the day. And it was a Friday, which meant three whole days without Mr. Fabiano. The weekend was ruined.

She drifted over to where Tommy Feathers used to sit. A photograph of Tommy hung on the wall, but Rachel turned away from the grinning face and glanced at his old desk. She reached down and quickly touched the surface, running her thumb over the place where a heart had been carved into the wood and the letters *T.F.* + *R.W.* crudely cut inside the heart.

Missy came into the room and stared at the blackboard.

"Oh, no, a sub," Missy said, reading. "What a bummer."

Rachel and Missy had been best friends since second grade. Before Rachel stopped talking, they'd get on the phone and lose track of time in deep talks about boys, music, religion, God, ghosts, ESP, telepathy. They agreed that it was possible to read another person's thoughts, if you were close enough.

Missy was fat. Rachel often wondered if Missy's own problems helped her to understand Rachel's. Missy knew what it was like to have kids point fingers, make nasty comments, whisper behind her back. She knew what it was like to have something eating at you from the inside.

More than anybody else Missy accepted Rachel's silence. Other kids got all nervous and chatty around Rachel: Not Missy. When they were together Missy didn't try to fill the dead space with lots of empty chitchat the way most kids did. The silence always felt light and easy between them.

Loud laughter outside the door. Karen and Jasmine raced into the room.

"I won!" Karen said, laughing and breathing hard.

"*They* won," Jasmine said, pointing. "Hi, Missy. Hey, Rachel."

Last fall when Rachel stopped talking she stopped smiling, too. Now she gave the girls a small wave as a gesture intended to mean "Hello." At the beginning of the year Rachel considered Karen and Jasmine close friends. After Rachel stopped talking, the other two girls still acted friendly toward her, but things were somehow different now.

"Anyway," Jasmine was saying, "I would've beat you if you hadn't tripped me."

"Tripped you?" The girls took seats next to each other on the other side of the room. "You tripped yourself."

Christopher Ransom lumbered into the room.

"I'm ready to go home now!" he announced, flopping down onto his desk and stretching out two big feet. Christopher's mother was president of the P.T.A. His father was a heart surgeon— Christopher liked to brag that his father "cut people up." He was rich, loud, and obnoxious.

Jessica and Vicki came in next. Rachel thought they looked a little funny together since Vicki was so short and Jessica was the tallest kid in the class.

"Oh, a sub," Jessica groaned, seeing the note on the blackboard.

"Fact." Christopher smirked. He rubbed his hands gleefully. "And what better way to end the week than tormenting some brain-damaged sub?"

Christopher's voice put Rachel on edge; the kid was annoying beyond belief. To help tune him out, she watched the rest of the class enter the room. Tim and Jordan ran in, laughing, with Robert and Corey right behind. Robert and Corey were part of a set of triplets; the third triplet, Josh, was in Mrs. Reilly's class. Then Rhonda came in and plopped down next to Missy.

"My last day!" Bastian shouted as he entered the room.

"I thought you said Monday was your last day," Karen said.

"My dad changed plans," Bastian said. "Farewell, peons! I am leaving you for the beaches of Hawaii!"

"You'll look great in a hula hula skirt," Jessica told him.

"You should talk, String Bean!" Bastian retorted. "Remember that time you wore a dress? I laughed so hard I almost peed in my pants!"

"Shut up, Bastian," Rhonda said.

Bastian had a mean streak, and Rachel didn't trust him. He had moved into town just before the beginning of sixth grade and immediately made his presence felt by teasing kids in class. He invented nasty little nicknames for just about everybody. Missy: Thunder Thighs. Vicki: The Shrimp. Jessica: String Bean. He called Tommy Feathers The Professor or, sometimes, Doctor Drool.

Sean O'Day walked into the room and quietly took his seat at the back of the room. He was slender with a pale, sleepy complexion. Rachel noticed that he was wearing the same Chicago Bulls T-shirt he'd worn the day before. Now he glanced at her shyly and busied himself digging into his backpack.

"You are my Sean-shine, my only Sean-shine," Christopher sang loudly. "You make me hap-peee . . . when skies are grayyyyy."

"Leave him alone," Bastian told him. "Not funny."

"Opinion." Christopher grinned.

Sean and Bastian had one thing in common: Sean's father, like Bastian's, had served in the Air Force. Sean's father had left the military years ago, but Bastian said that didn't matter. Air Force is Air Force, once and forever.

Sean was the one kid Bastian never picked on. And he wouldn't let anybody else pick on him, either.

The newest kid in class, Sky Reed, came in last. He had moved from southern California in January. Tall and lanky, Sky had an earring and wore his blond hair in a long braid. Bastian teased him about the earring; he and Sky got into a fight on the playground. Nobody won the fight, but Bastian's lip got cut, and after that nobody teased Sky about the earring or anything else.

"Where's the sub?" Tim asked, drumming on his desk. He was another boy who always made Rachel edgy. "You watch the high school baseball game? They kicked South Side's butt. Anybody watch Star Trek last night? That was pretty freaky. Hey, so where's the sub?"

"Sub is short for subhuman," Bastian said. "Looks like she ditched us."

Christopher started to sing: "We got ditched by a ditzy sub-marine, a ditzy sub-marine . . . "

"Not funny," Vicki said. "Not even close."

"Opinion," Christopher replied smugly.

Mr. Peacock came over the loudspeaker to make the morning announcements.

"GOOD MORNING," he said. TODAY IS FRIDAY, APRIL TWENTY-EIGHTH."

"Fact," Christopher said.

"IT'S A BEAUTIFUL SPRING DAY," Mr. Peacock said.

"Opinion." Christopher smirked.

"Shut up!" Rhonda told him.

Mr. Peacock proceeded to run through the day's business. Sign-ups for Jazz Band. No cheerleading practice. Track meet next Thursday. Bring in cans for the food drive. Important reminder: No hats allowed in school.

"PLEASE STAND FOR THE PLEDGE," Mr. Peacock said.

Kids looked around, unsure of what to do. Bastian got up first. That was one thing his father had taught him—you stand for the flag. Always. When Bastian stood up the other boys started getting out of their seats. Soon the whole class was pledging in ragged unison: ". . . one nation . . . under God . . . with liberty . . . and justice . . . for all."

They sat down. Still no sub.

"This lady must be totally clueless," Bastian said, loudly cracking his knuckles.

"Opinion," Christopher said.

29

"It could be a man," Jessica said.

"Fact," Christopher put in.

"I'm begging you," Rhonda told Christopher. "Shut up!"

"Attendance," Karen said from the front of the room. "Who's absent?"

"I am," Christopher said.

"I wish," Rhonda retorted.

"John's out," Bastian said. "Really."

"David's not coming in," Robert said. "He got an asthma attack yesterday."

"Melinda's sick, too," Vicki said.

Rachel watched Karen fill out the attendance, checking off *present* or *absent*. Her eyes lit on Tommy Feathers's empty desk. There was no place on any attendance form to check off *dead*.

"How many hot lunches?" Karen said.

"Who elected *you* teacher?" Bastian demanded.

"She's class president," Jessica pointed out. "That's her job."

"Hot lunch?" Karen asked again, ignoring Bastian.

"What are they having?" Corey asked.

"You don't want to know," Rhonda said. "Greaseball pizza. Guaranteed ninety percent soaked in grease!"

Karen counted eight hot lunches, five chocolate milks, and three whites.

"Okay, who wants to bring it to the office?" Karen asked.

"Me! Me!"

Rachel thought it was funny the way everybody raised their hands, by habit, even without a teacher. It made her want to smile, but she didn't. Rachel watched Karen standing there, deciding whom to pick. She really admired Karen. The girl was a born leader. Her neat black bangs and dark eyes gave her a no-nonsense look. People took her seriously.

"Come to think of it," Karen said, "I'll go myself."

"No fair!" Tim moaned.

"Hey," Jessica said. "Don't forget to tell them about the sub."

"Don't worry," Karen said, bouncing out of the room.

"I will give a lecture while she's gone," Christopher announced.

"No you won't," Rhonda told him.

"Why not?" Tim shot back. "Ever hear of the First Amendment? He has the right to free speech."

"He has the right to be quiet," Rhonda retorted.

Rachel folded her hands. It was more than that, much more. Not just the right to *be* silent but the right to *remain* silent. It was a right protected by federal law.

31

——— Main Office ———

Helen Pierce had been the school secretary for nearly thirty years but had never gotten used to the frantic pace of the mornings. She took a sip of coffee and closed her eyes, trying to think. There was a nagging splinter in her mind, someone she was supposed to call, something she had to do, but what? Who?

"My mind is a sieve," she said to Shelley Fields, a parent who often helped out in the office.

"I can't imagine why." Shelley laughed. "I mean, it's so peaceful around here!"

Helen grunted and got up to pour herself another cup of coffee. Already it had been ONE OF THOSE MORNINGS full of crises–Peggy Ransom's tirade, a boy who swore at a bus driver, two kids who had to be sent home because of head lice, a leaky pipe in the gym. On top of that, an iguana had escaped from its cage in one of the science rooms. And it was barely 9 A.M. On mornings like this she pictured her mind as a glass that has broken and shattered into countless tiny transparent pieces so small you can't find them until you step on one. And get cut.

Back at her desk she went over the phone messages, one by one. There were six messages, and she'd taken care of them all. Irwin Peacock opened his door a crack and stuck out his head.

"Have a minute?" he asked her. "We need to plan for the assembly this afternoon. The story-teller. There's going to be local press."

"All right," Helen said. She turned to Shelley. "Can you cover the phones for ten minutes?"

"Sure thing," Shelley replied.

Helen disappeared inside Mr. Peacock's office. A minute later Karen Ballard appeared in the doorway. Shelley knew Karen—everyone did. Karen was one of the brightest, most confident students in the entire school, although today she looked a little unsure of herself.

"Hello there, Karen," Shelley said. "What can I do for you?"

Karen hesitated a moment, then put a piece of paper on the desk. "Lunch count and attendance sheet for 6-238."

"Thank you. Anything else?"

"No, that's all," Karen said. She smiled and hurried out of the room.

9:00 A.M.

—— KIDS RULE!!! ——

Rachel's silence had changed her in unexpected ways. Without her voice she had learned how to watch, how to tune in to a million little things she had never before noticed. She saw the little gifts Rhonda and Jasmine gave Karen to compete for her friendship. A few days ago Rachel spied a secret glance and shy smile between Sky and Vicki (of all people!) during math. Today she noticed Bastian chewing his nails–something he never did.

She glanced over at Sean. He had his head down on the desk; she wondered if he was asleep. She took out her book, *A Beginner's Flight Manual,* and began to read.

The bones of birds are hollow but strong. This hollowness helps them to fly. It is interesting to note that airplane wings are mostly empty, filled with nothing but air.

Rachel liked this passage so much she read it

again. The words described exactly how she felt this morning. Strong and hollow. Filled with air and silence. Just itching to fly.

"Okay," Karen said, flitting into the room. Her eyes were bright, cheeks slightly flushed as if she'd run all the way back. "Still no sub, huh?"

"The Case of the Missing Sub," Robert said.

"Yeah, we're, like, orphans!" Tim cried plaintively.

"Speak for yourself," Bastian said. "I know who my mother is!"

Karen went to Mr. Fabiano's desk and picked up a folder.

"Must be the lesson plans Mr. Fab left for the sub," she said. "Here's the spelling test. Might as well get that over with, right?"

"Better do *some*thing before we die of boredom," Tim muttered.

"I'll give the spelling words," Jessica said.

"Why you?" Christopher demanded.

"Because I always get a hundred on spelling tests," Jessica retorted.

It was no different from any other spelling test, Rachel thought, as kids groaned and muttered and snapped open binders and pulled out blank sheets of lined paper. Jessica stood in the center of the three tables, slowly reading the words twice and using them in a sentence just as Mr. Fabiano always did.

"Perceive . . . perceive . . . Many people perceive professional athletes as rich, spoiled, self-ish individuals."

"Not!" Bastian yelled.

"Quiet!" Jessica said. "The next word is sou-venir . . . souvenir . . . When Christopher went to Disney World, his father bought him a stuffed Mickey Mouse as a souvenir of the trip."

"Hardy har har," Christopher said.

It was 9:30 by the time they had finished the test, handed out the answer key, corrected their answers, compared scores, and written their mis-spelled words in the back of their writing folders.

"So what do we do now?" Robert asked, slumping in his seat.

"I'm taking a nap," Bastian announced, lying down on the floor. "Wake me when somebody shows up. *If* somebody shows up."

"Show-off," Rhonda said. "You wouldn't do this if Mr. Fab was here."

"This is getting a little freaky," Tim said.

"Welcome to the Twilight Zone," Christopher put in.

"Yeah, what's the *deal?*" Vicki asked. She turned to look at Karen. "What did they say about the sub when you went to the office?"

"Nothing," Karen said.

"Nothing?"

"Nope," Karen said, shrugging. "They didn't say a thing. Because I didn't tell them."

Bastian sat up. Everyone looked at Karen.

"Didn't tell them?" Rhonda asked. "Why not?"

"Don't you guys get it?" Karen asked. She leaned forward and snapped her fingers, eyes bright with excitement. "There's obviously been some kind of major mix-up. They *forgot* about us."

"So . . . " Rhonda said.

"So I started thinking: Why tell anybody?" Karen said. "I figured: Let's run the class ourselves."

"Yesss!" Christopher said, making a fist. He jumped up and started goose-stepping across the floor.

"We can do it!" Karen said. "I know we can!"

Kids looked around at one another, smiling, giggling nervously. Missy looked over at Rachel; they raised their eyebrows at the exact same time.

"Very true," Jasmine agreed. "I mean, if we can't run this class for one day, we're a total bunch of losers."

"I'm with you," Jordan said.

"Me, too," said Robert and Corey.

"Count me in," Bastian said. "KIDS RULE! KIDS RULE! KIDS RULE!"

"Sure, why not?" Vicki asked.

"Why not?" Jessica asked. "Are you kidding? It's illegal, that's why not!"

Everybody stared at her.

"Opinion," Christopher said.

"Yeah, are you sure?" Karen asked.

"It's wrong, it's dangerous, somebody could get hurt," Jessica said, glaring at Karen. "Mr. Fab would want us to go down to the office and tell them right now. I can't believe you didn't tell them!"

Rachel wrote something on a piece of paper and handed it to Missy.

"Wait a sec," Missy said. "Rachel wants to say something."

"Ah," Bastian said. "The Silent Pilot speaks!"

"Be quiet!" Missy told him. She took Rachel's note and read it aloud: *I wouldn't be so sure of that.*

"Oh, sure," Jessica said, making a face at Rachel. "Sure, Mr. Fab would just love the idea of us being totally unsupervised all day while he's gone. Give me a break! This is the dumbest, stupidest, most asinine idea I've ever heard of."

"Opinion." Christopher smirked.

Missy picked up another note from Rachel and read it aloud: *I think Mr. Fabiano would want us to think and talk about it and then decide. He's always talking about moral decisions.*

"I don't believe this." Jessica shook her head.

"Look, Mr. Fab isn't here," Jasmine pointed out. "We have to do what *we* think is right. Right?"

"I'm for it," Sky said quietly.

"KIDS RULE!" Bastian and Tim chanted. "KIDS RULE! KIDS RULE! KIDS RULE!"

"Shush!" Missy said. "We should vote."

"We should *not* vote!" Jessica said, banging her desk. "It's the most demented idea I've heard since my sister tried to put the cat in the dryer!"

"What are you worried about?" Bastian asked. "What could possibly happen? This school is crawling with teachers."

"Fact," Christopher said.

"Let's vote and get on with it," Karen said. "Who votes we should run the class ourselves today?"

An instant crop of raised hands.

"Who votes no?"

Jessica stuck her long arm straight up into the air.

"Fourteen to one," Karen said.

"Fact!" Christopher grinned and crossed his arms.

They all looked at Jessica.

"Sorry, String Bean, looks like you lose," Bastian said. "You gonna go squeal?"

"Shut your face!" Jessica hissed at him. "What I do, and when I do it, is none of your business!"

"Hey, let's all chill," Jasmine said.

For a moment no one did anything but breathe.

"Okay, so what next?" Vicki asked quietly.

"Party time!" Tim cried.

"Flashdrafts," Missy said, pointing at the schedule printed on the blackboard. "Writing."

"Oh, come on," Bastian moaned.

Vicki went over to the tape player. Soon a mellow jazz began to fill the classroom. Mr. Fab believed in a daily schedule with as few surprises as possible: spelling, Flashdrafts, music/computer lab (one every other day), math, Connections (more writing), lunch, D.E.A.R., Exploration, science. To keep things predictable he had certain rituals, like playing music during writing time. Rachel hadn't liked the music at first. But with time she found that it got her in the mood to write and actually helped her concentration.

"This is stupid," Bastian said. "I don't feel like writing. I'm not in the mood."

"Morning time is writing time," Vicki said, repeating one of Mr. Fabiano's favorite lines.

"Shut up, Shrimp," Bastian muttered. Vicki was the shortest girl in the sixth grade.

"Hey, that's a put-down," Jasmine said, glaring at him.

"Oooh," Bastian mocked, raising his hands. "A put-down! Gee whiz! That's bad!"

"I don't know about you guys," Karen said, "but I'm going to write."

"I can't believe this!" Bastian sighed.

Jessica sat at her desk, arms folded. After a minute she snapped open her binder and pulled out a blank piece of paper.

The minute Rachel closed her eyes she got a picture of Tommy Feathers, the way he used to grin at her whenever she glanced his way. She didn't have to wonder how Tommy would have voted. He would have voted with the majority because Tommy wanted people to like him.

Tommy wasn't a very good writer, but he liked to write. At the beginning of writing time he would often lean over to Rachel and whisper: *I'm gonna write a story for you.* He hummed loudly while he worked, and after about ten minutes he'd pass his paper over to her. *That's for you, Rachel.* He gave her dozens of stories like this.

Every day she threw them away. She hadn't kept a single one.

She tried not to think about that now. She tried hard to put Tommy's face and voice out of her mind.

Around her Rachel could see other kids stretching and fidgeting as they started to write. She took out her favorite pen, opened to a blank piece of notebook paper, and tried to clear her head.

Writing words is like flying, Rachel thought. *Words aren't solid. Words are lighter than air. But even so, they can sometimes give you a lift.*

———— Flashdrafts ————

Rachel

Dear Mr. Fabiano,

Mom is so worried about me. She says: "Pick up your voice if you happen to find it on the way to school." Last month she gave me a card and told me to open it on the bus.

"You are like a magic caterpillar," she wrote. "You surprised everyone by spinning a strange and beautiful cocoon, a chrysalis of silence. Soon you will emerge with new wings. And we'll be here when you do. We'll be here to watch you fly."

What Mom doesn't understand is that my voice *isn't* lost. I've learned that I can find it whenever I want as soon as I pick up my pen. The moment I start writing words I can hear the sound of my voice on the paper.

In so many ways it was you who helped to make that happen. You never pushed me to talk like lots of other people did. You said: "Writers cultivate silence." You said: "You'll speak when you're ready." You said: "Your writing is full of voice."

Sean

Once my father took me hunting and it was exciting. At the beginning of the year Rachel told me she hates hunting. But I would never shoot a animal except if a bear charged because bears look friendly but they can be real nasty.

I don't want to go home after school, not today. My father might be there still sleeping it off so I can't watch TV unless I turn it down way low. Sometimes he's up and that can be worse. Or if he's gone Darlene is there and sometimes she bothers me while I'm watching TV. Most times she's okay but sometimes she says dumb things and then I just ignore her and go outside into the woods. I do that a lot. I go out into the woods. Way back into the deepest woods.

I doubt most people would dare go that far deep as I go. I pretend I'm hunting. Sometimes I wish I had a dog that would come with me. But I'm not afraid to go out there alone. There are beautiful places in the woods, like rooms with high high ceilings. You walk into a clearing and it feels like being in a room with trees all around and light coming through the windows. And it's quiet.

Sometimes I take a nap back there. I think it

would be a place I'd like to show Rachel sometimes, those rooms in the trees. We could walk
around together, maybe sit down and eat a
snack. I don't care how quiet she'd be. Who
cares if she never says one word?

Jasmine

Karen thinks I should be a doctor when I
grow up so we could have a practice together–
Dad thinks I should be an engineer. Freddy Labo
says I'm pretty enough to be a model–but he's in
eleventh grade and I can't tell if he's serious, or
kidding, or just being fresh.

What I really want to do is be a wife and
mother and stay home with my kids. Some kids
say that's a waste of time–but, believe me, it's
not.

I love children–and I believe it's important to
raise them right–especially in a world like ours.
Being a good mother is a full-time job. I might
even want to teach them myself–at home.

Bastian

Dear Mr. Fab,

Today's my last day at school. I know I told you
I'd be here on Monday but Dad changed his mind
so we're going to Hawaii tomorrow morning.

My puppy is getting shipped to Hawaii on the

plane tonight. They have a special cage for him, and Mom has to give him special medicine so he'll sleep most of the flight. They are putting him in Quarantine for four months. The military does that for all dogs who come to Hawaii from the rest of the U.S. It's a stupid rule but Dad says there are no exceptions. At least I'll get to visit him every day when he's in Quarantine.

Since you're out today I probably won't get to see you again. I know I wasn't exactly an angel in class, but I want to say that you've been a good teacher. You never made me feel like an "Air Force Brat" like some other teachers did.

Missy

Tim said: "We're like orphans." He was just kidding but that made me think about a movie, about how they started Boys' Town, for runaway kids. There was one part that made me cry, when this boy was carrying his little brother on his back, and a man asked: Isn't he heavy? And the boy (who was carrying the little boy) answered: He's not heavy, he's my brother.

I think, today, we are like orphans, not all ways, but some. We have to help each other, since we don't have any teacher to watch over us. Or even a sub. We're on our own.

There's still some writing time left, so I think I'll just copy the story list on the wall:

STORIES . . .

1) are unique as snowflakes. No two are exactly alike.

2) contain small details that often turn out to be important.

3) involve limits: particular characters in a particular place and time.

4) put characters in difficult situations.

5) force characters to make moral choices.

6) contain a problem or conflict that often gets worse before it gets better.

7) connect the ordinary with the extraordinary.

8) usually contain a surprise. (Or two.)

9) sometimes turn on a "moment of silence."

10) rarely turn out the way you expect.

Music ——————

"Are we going to do a share?" Vicki asked.

"Can't!" Jordan said, pointing at the clock. "Computer lab!"

"No, we did computer lab yesterday," Karen said. "Music."

"Fact," Christopher said. "We'd better go before they come hunting for us."

"Just go?" Jasmine asked. "With no teacher? You don't think that's sort of . . . obvious?"

"Not if we're super quiet in the halls," Karen said.

"Yes, Miss Ballard, Sir!" Christopher said. He saluted her smartly.

"Very funny," Karen retorted. "Hey, I mean it. We've got to make zero noise or somebody's going to notice. We've got to be *invisible.*"

"Better suck in your gut," Bastian said, nudging Missy.

"Leave her alone!" Rhonda said, smacking him on the arm.

47

"I was just kidding," Bastian said. "Can't you take a joke?"

"It's not funny, you idiot!"

"Quiet!" Karen said.

The kids filed out of the classroom. Rachel walked along the hallway of polished linoleum, long and perfectly smooth. For a miniature airplane, this hall would make a perfect runway for taking off or landing.

She watched the line of students ahead of her. They all kept their eyes facing straight ahead as they filed down the hall. Even their footsteps seemed strangely muted as they moved over the linoleum, past the other three sixth-grade classrooms, and down the stairs. The column made a smooth right onto the central corridor, and then another right into the All-Purpose Room that was used for music.

Inside, Mrs. Ickeringill, the music teacher, was waiting for them at the piano. She was a stocky red-faced woman wearing glasses and a button that read: MUSIC IS MY LIFE.

"Welcome," she said. "Please take your places, boys and girls. Chop chop. Come now, we don't have much time."

Class 6-238 assembled on the riser, sopranos to the left, altos to the right. Rachel had no intention of singing but she took her place with the altos as she always did. Wedging herself between Missy and Jasmine, Rachel got a mental image of Tommy Feathers, face bright and eager, singing in last year's winter concert. He sure loved to sing. It didn't seem to matter to him in the least that he "couldn't carry a tune in a bucket," as they say.

Mrs. Ickeringill played a few piano notes to the song, a stirring melody with lyrics taken from the poem on the Statue of Liberty. Rachel stood quietly as the kids began to sing around her. Today their voices combined to make a clear strong sound:

> *Give me your tired your poooooor*
> *Your huddled masses yearning to breathe*
>   *freeeee*
> *The wretched refuse of your teeming shoooore*
> *Sennnnd theeese*
> *The homeless, tempest-tossed to meeee*
> *I lift my lamp beside the gooooolden doooor*

"Wonderful!" Mrs. Ickeringill cried. She sat up and looked at them, surprised. "You've got spirit today! You've got *juice!* Again! Let's take it from the top!"

They sang it again and the song sounded even more beautiful than before, so much so that Rachel could feel the beginnings of a sound rising from some deep buried place at the bottom of her chest, itching to join in, and it was everything she could do to keep that sound down.

───────── **Snack** ─────────

Back in Room 238 kids took out their snacks along with their math books. In her backpack Rachel found carrots and—yes!—a bag of vinegar-and-salt-flavored potato chips. She knew the chips were bad for her, full of fat, laced with chemicals and dye, almost green-colored, but she didn't care. And today Mom had given her an extra-large bag. She opened it, took out a bunch, and offered it to Missy.

"Oh, I can't," Missy sighed. "My mom's got me on another diet."

Rachel glanced beyond Missy's desk to where Sean was sitting. She noticed that today there was no snack on his desk. While the kids around him chatted and ate, Sean busied himself with rummaging through his desk. Rachel looked at Missy, offered the bag of chips, and motioned with her eyes at Sean.

"Oh, yeah, sure," Missy said, taking the bag

from Rachel. "Hey, Sean, you want some of these? From Rachel."

"Thanks," he mumbled. He took a bunch of chips from the bag and passed it back to Rachel.

A month ago Rachel had had to meet with the school psychologist during snack time. She'd bring a small bag of carrots or celery and sit outside Mr. Snickenberger's office until he called her to come in. He was a tall bearded man who wore bright ugly ties, but he always had a fresh bowl of salt-and-vinegar potato chips on his desk. She'd munch those chips while he asked questions. *How would you describe your relationship with your mother? How long have your parents been divorced? Did you become interested in flying around the time when your father moved out? How did you feel about Tommy Feathers and how do you think he felt about you? Did he ever touch you, or try to kiss you?* Sometimes she'd answer his questions with written notes, but mostly she just listened, nodded or shook her head, and savored those chips, the delicious chemical tang they left on her tongue.

I don't like him, she wrote to her mother one night while sitting at the kitchen table.

Why not? Can't stand those gaudy ties?

He gives me the creeps. He acts like he knows stuff about me I don't know.

Mr. Snickenberger was pleasant with her for the first few weeks. But as time passed he began losing patience with her silence. One day he asked her a series of questions, and when she didn't reply the man suddenly exploded.

I'll tell you what I *think,* he said with an angry face. *I think your obsession with flying is your attempt to fly away from your problems. Well, it won't work, young lady! One thing you need to learn is, you can't run away from your life! That's a lesson you'd better learn sooner than later!*

That marked her last session with Mr. Snickenberger. But even though she stopped seeing him, she had no intention of giving up those salt-and-vinegar potato chips. Now she took one last handful of chips and passed the bag to Missy with a gesture that said: "Finished."

"Here," Missy said, handing the bag to Sean. "You can have the rest."

Rachel saw the pleasure in Sean's eyes, and was glad she'd left him a lot.

11:18 A.M.

——— Visitors ———

"Let's put some music on!" Christopher said.

"Yeah! Rock 'n' roll!"

"Better rock quietly," Karen told him, "unless you want a bunch of teachers crawling all over us."

"This is stupid!" Bastian said. "We've got no teacher, but we're sitting here doing geometry! We're acting like we're on detention! Let's *do* something! Who's stopping us?"

"You–"

Knock! Knock!

Rachel stared at the door. When it opened, Katie Bretz sailed into the room. Katie was in Mrs. Reilly's class. She was dressed in a blue jumper with matching blue socks and a tiny blue ribbon in her blond hair. Katie seemed a little bit preppy–perfect posture, every hair in place–but everyone agreed she was a talented actress. She had already appeared in two commercials. They were dumb commercials for laundry detergent, but still, she had been on TV.

"Mrs. Reilly needs the book club orders," she said.

"Okay," Karen said, taking a large envelope off Mr. Fabiano's desk. "Here you go."

"Where's Mr. Fab?"

"He's . . . out at the moment," Karen explained.

"Out?" Katie glanced around the classroom.

"Yeah, we're supposed to have a sub," Tim explained, "but the sub didn't show up, either. We're just sort of winging it today."

Bastian elbowed Tim, hard.

"Yeah, right!" Katie said. With a toss of her blond hair she breezed out of the room.

"That was stupid," Jasmine told Tim. "Extremely stupid. I mean, why not just announce it to the whole school?"

"She didn't believe me," Tim said, giggling. "Did you see that? She didn't believe me! It's just too unbelievable!"

Another knock on the door, louder this time. This time Morgan Hasshagen strolled in. He had a crewcut and an Orlando Magic T-shirt. Morgan's father ran the local funeral home. Morgan was so small he looked more like a fourth grader than a sixth grader.

"Mr. Fab?" he asked, glancing around.

"He's not here," Karen said smoothly.

"You got a sub . . . ?" Morgan asked, still looking.

"What do you need?" Karen asked him.

"Hey, where is everybody?" Morgan asked. His eyes darted from one side of the room to another, and he looked so funny Rachel had to work hard to squelch a smile. Karen giggled, and a few other kids joined in.

"We're all here," Jasmine said. "Alone."

"Fact," Christopher said.

"Yeah, right." Morgan smiled. "You lie."

"You're right, it's a lie," Karen said. "So what do you need?"

"Are you guys really . . . alone?" Morgan asked.

"The sub never showed up," Karen explained, nodding calmly. "Guess they figured we didn't need any teacher today. And it turns out they're right."

Morgan stared at her. He knew Karen was not the kind of girl who went around making up stories. His expression slowly changed from skepticism to wide-eyed disbelief.

"Really?" He looked out at the class. "You guys got nobody here? You didn't tell anybody?"

"You tell anybody and you die!" Rhonda told him.

"This is so cool!" Morgan leaped up onto Mr. Fab's desk and started doing a fast boogie-woogie.

"How mature," Rhonda said. "Get off there, you jerk!"

Morgan jumped off and pulled open one of the drawers in Mr. Fabiano's desk.

"What do you think you're doing?"

"Candy," Morgan said. "Mr. Fab keeps a stash down here."

"Hey!" Bastian jumped up out of his seat. "You take any of Mr. Fab's candy, I'll break your arm!"

"Okay, okay," Morgan said, holding up both hands, palms out. He picked up a shiny rock on Mr. Fabiano's desk, a cubic piece of pyrite, and tossed it into the air. Rachel drew a quick sharp breath. That had been Tommy Feathers's favorite rock.

"Put that down!" Missy said.

"Jeez!" Morgan said. "You guys sure are jumpy today!"

"We don't like other people messing with our stuff," Bastian said.

Now Morgan started slinking around the classroom, grinning, looking carefully at everything.

"Don't you have to get back to your class?" Jessica asked.

"Not really," Morgan said. When he spotted all the opened math books on the desks his face went all bug-eyed. "Don't tell me you guys are actually *working!* With no teacher? What a bunch of wusses!"

"Getting our work done now so we can party all afternoon," Christopher told him. He leaned back and loudly cracked his knuckles.

"And you're not invited!" Tim said.

"You're starting to get a little annoying," Karen told Morgan. "What exactly do you want?"

"Mrs. Kiefer needs the American history book. Teacher's edition."

"I'm not sure where that is," Karen said. "I'll look for it and bring it down. Just promise you won't tell any teachers till after school. Promise!"

"Oh sure, I'm gonna go squeal to my teacher," Morgan said, giving her a sour look. He leaped up onto Mr. Fabiano's desk again and did another quick boogie-woogie. "This is soooo cooool."

"Goodbye," Karen said. She pulled him off the desk and pushed him out the door.

Jasmine had to search all through the supply closet before she finally dug out the history book.

"Here it is," she said. Without a word, Sean O'Day got up and took it from her.

"I'll bring it," he said softly.

"Okay," Jasmine said.

Sean's stomach felt queasy, with those vinegary potato chips on top of the soda on top of the candy bar. Maybe a walk would help settle it down before he could get a hot meal at lunch.

Usually Sean got a special feeling, a peculiar kind of airiness, whenever he left a classroom to walk in the halls. Sean loved those few minutes when you could go *on your own* to the bathroom. Those were the only moments in the whole school day when he felt really free. Unseen. He always made a point of walking slowly, trying to make those few moments of school freedom last as long as possible.

But today leaving the class was different. He left a classroom where no teacher was watching and went out into the halls where a teacher might see him. It felt strange and he walked faster than usual to Mrs. Kiefer's classroom.

He knocked. Mrs. Kiefer was standing at the blackboard.

"Here," he said, handing her the history book.

"Tell Mr. Fabiano thank you," Mrs. Kiefer said. She was a thin woman with a pasty complexion, and she didn't look particularly happy. He was glad he had Mr. Fab for a teacher.

Sean nodded.

"Oh, that's right, he's out today, isn't he? Well, thank your sub."

"Okay," Sean mumbled as he edged to the door. On the way out he spotted Morgan Hasshagen waving like a maniac from the back of the room.

* * *

58

Music was playing when Sean returned to Room 238. A song by the Counting Crows, turned down low. Sean looked at the schedule on the board: 11:30, Connections. Writing again. Sean took his seat and glanced over at Rachel. He tried to catch her eye, but she was deep into her writing. Everyone was.

——— **Connections** ———

Bastian couldn't write. He sat staring out the window at a huge billowing cloud rushing against the blue sky. He was trying hard not to worry about Barkley, about the Quarantine, but he couldn't help it. More than anything he wanted to be home with his puppy.

Barkley will be okay, Mom had said before he left for school. *Every day thousands of dogs fly in airplanes all over the world. He'll be all right.*

It wasn't the flight that worried Bastian. True, the puppy would be alone, flying by himself in the cargo hold of some jet, but he would probably sleep through most of the flight. It was the next part that Bastian hated to think about. In Honolulu the puppy would be taken to a special place for quarantined animals. Bastian pictured some kind of animal jail: cages, iron bars.

Bastian got up, walked to the bookcase, pulled

out the fat dictionary, and turned to the Qs. He found it on page 1474.

Quarantine: a place where persons, animals, or plants having contagious diseases are kept in isolation to prevent the diseases from spreading. . . .

He slammed the book shut. Contagious diseases! It was stupid and cruel to quarantine a perfectly healthy puppy for four months for absolutely no reason! He opened the thesaurus and thumbed through it until he found it. *Quarantine,* verb. *Synonyms:*

> *Separate.*
> *Hospitalize.*
> *Keep apart.*
> *Isolate.*

* * *

Sean's stomach felt a little better now. He loved this time of day, late morning, when the room began to warm up. Today it was cloudy, the skies threatening rain, but on some days just before lunch a shaft of sunlight reached into the back of the class and put him in its spotlight. It was so peaceful to sit quietly wrapped in that bright warm cocoon.

Sean closed his eyes. The image of Darlene entered his mind. She was much younger than his mother, with blond hair and a pretty smile. Dad worked the three-to-eleven shift as a security guard at a computer factory. Most nights he stopped at the bar on the way home, so he rarely got home until way after midnight. Darlene was usually in the apartment, reading magazines or watching TV, when Sean came home from school. Some days she ignored him; some days she tried to boss him around. Other days she made him feel kind of funny, the way she followed him through the house, asking: *You got any girls at school that are sweet on you? Hmmm?*

Sean glanced over at Rachel. She was still writing. Sean picked up his pen and started to write. He wrote fast, his face close to the paper.

She never talks. But I wonder if maybe sometimes she closes her door tight and hums a little. Or whistles a little tune. Or maybe late at night when everybody's sleeping she lets out a couple words real soft just to see if she can still do it. I wonder if it's all scratchy and creaky. I bought an old fishing reel for two dollars off Dad's friend Roger and it was so rusty me and Dad had to oil it up with about a gallon of WD-40 until the crank turned nice and smooth.

Last month me and Dad found three baby kittens that were trapped in a trash can. Dad said he didn't know how they got in there but somebody sealed the lid real tight and I heard them

*when I walked by and pulled off the lid. A white
one, and two mixed. And no mother around. And
crying like the end of the world. We gave them
some milk and then I held them in my lap. They
kept crying and licking me and their tongues
were like sandpaper. It took a long time to get
them calmed down. Darlene's allergic to cats so
we had to give the kittens away. We found good
homes for all of them. But I wish we could've kept
one.*

"We better stop if we're gonna share any of
these."

The kids blinked and looked up from their
desks. The voice had come from Karen.

"Yes, Mrs. Fabiano," Bastian said in a high
voice.

"C'mon," Karen said, ignoring him and lead-
ing the way to the back of the room. The other
kids got up and found seats in the Share Area.

Share time in Mr. Fabiano's class was always
the same. Kids took turns reading their writing,
moving clockwise from Mr. Fab, who always sat
by the corner of the bookcase. Today that spot
was held by Tim.

"Tim?" Karen asked.

"No way," Tim said. "I'm not reading today–I'm
on strike."

"Robert?"

"What the heck," Robert said. "I'll go."

He cleared his throat, pounded on his chest, and read:

I have been thinking about how we don't have any teacher today. I remember this science fiction movie I saw one time when John slept over and there were these aliens who were using humans in this town for an experiment. The aliens had planted these tiny computers in the humans' brains, only the humans had no idea they were being controlled from outer space.

That's like today. Everybody's acting like we're getting away with something by being totally free. Well, I disagree. I would not be surprised if today is like an experiment for how kids would act without any teacher. Mr. Fab left us a note but I don't totally trust him. I don't totally trust any grownups.

Robert stopped.

"Is that finished?" Missy asked.

"That's all I got," he said, putting down his paper.

"Why would Mr. Fab do an experiment on us?" Tim wanted to know. "Do you have, like, a theory?"

"Maybe it's not Mr. Fab," Robert said, shrugging. "Maybe it's Mr. Peacock. Maybe he's trying to show kids can't control themselves. You know, so they can make more rules in the school."

"I seriously doubt that," Karen said. "But any-way, we can prove him wrong. We *are* proving him wrong. Christopher?"

"Yes, I shall read my masterpiece!" Christopher declared proudly. "You will now hear the Legend of Sir Francis Brave Fart!"

"Braveheart?" Robert asked.

"No, Brave *Fart!*" Christopher said and started reading.

On the night before the great battle Sir Francis Brave Fart came to dinner with a legion of other fearless knights. As he sat down on a chair he suddenly farted and the chair exploded in a cloud of foul smoke.

The boys cracked up.

"You moron," Jasmine said.

"Opinion!" Christopher giggled. He read:

The other knights were stunned and excited. They had finally found a secret new weapon that might work in their bloody war against the all-powerful Dark Knight!

"That's all I have so far," Christopher said. "Stay tuned for the next adventure of Sir Francis Brave Fart!"

"That would make a great movie," Tim said. "I'd go see it."

"I wouldn't," Rhonda said.

"Jessica?" Karen said. "You're next."

"Okay," Jessica said, "but you guys won't like it."

She read:

I read about these parents who left their kids alone in the house for almost a week while they went on vacation. The kids were both under ten years old. The parents got arrested when they came home. What did they expect?

Another time two brothers were home alone. They went into their father's bedroom to look at their father's gun. The gun cabinet was unlocked. The gun was loaded. Stories like this are so predictable. How can anybody be shocked when the gun went off and killed one of the kids?

That is what is happening today in this room. We are playing with a loaded gun. Someone could bring a lawsuit against the school for what is happening in this class today. I know this because my father is a lawyer. A good lawyer would argue that the school was negligent by leaving us alone and unsupervised, not just for a few minutes, but for the whole school day. How could any jury possibly disagree?

We are not equipped to deal with running our own class. Doing math or writing is no big deal. But what if a fight starts? What if someone has an epileptic seizure? What if—

"What if someone farts?!" Christopher interrupted her.

"Kindly shut up," Rhonda told him.

"Yeah, nobody interrupted you!" Karen told him. She looked at Jessica and nodded. "Go on."

"That's about it," she said, glaring at Christopher.

"You end all your paragraphs with questions," Robert said. He leaned over and pointed at her paper. "Ever notice that?"

"Hmm," Jessica said, looking down.

"Could your father sue *us*?" Corey asked.

"I doubt it," Jessica said. "We're all minors."

"Fact," Christopher put in.

"We have time for a couple more," Karen said. "Missy?"

"Uh uh," she said, clutching her paper against her. Missy never shared her writing.

"Okay. Rachel?"

Rachel handed her paper to Missy. Missy cleared her voice and began to read:

I was thinking about when we read Hatchet *by Gary Paulsen, at the beginning of the year. Brian is flying on a bush plane to visit his father in Canada but the pilot has a heart attack and Brian has to take over the controls. He learns to crash-land the plane and survives the wreck. After that he has to learn to survive in the wilderness.*

It's sort of like what's happening today. True,

nobody had a heart attack around here. And it's true that we are not in the Canadian wilderness. But we are trying to see if we can survive on our own without any grownups. I halfway think we're doing the right thing, but I halfway think Jessica's right. It is dangerous. Anything could happen.

"The first sensible words I've heard all day," Jessica said, smiling at Rachel. "Other than mine, of course."

"*Hatchet* was cool," Bastian said. "Remember when the kid ate the raw turtle egg? That was nasty!"

"We have time for one more," Karen asked. "Sean?"

Sean shook his head.

"Okay. Sky?"

Nobody in the class really knew Sky. He'd arrived at the school in January, and he still hadn't made any close friends. Rachel often saw him at recess, standing alone on the playground or sitting by himself. He hardly ever talked in class, and he had never once read aloud any of his writing. Now Sky looked down at his paper and shrugged. With a soft voice he started to read.

I was thinking about when Mr. Fab told us on Monday about that time he was rushing his pregnant sister to the hospital. He knew he was doing something he'd never forget and he said to himself: I'M INSIDE A STORY.

That reminded me of one time I was surfing in California. This monster swell came and I caught it perfectly. For a few seconds I was inside the curl of the wave.

It was my first time ever and it didn't last very long but I'll remember every detail of that ride till the day I die. The board under my toes. The water a half foot thick all around me. The blue-green light coming through the water. The hissing sound of the wave. So much spray flying in my face I could barely see. My ears popping from the change of air pressure. It was an awesome rush, like nothing else in the world. I felt happy and scared, and the whole time I kept saying to myself: HEY, I'M IN IT! I'M INSIDE THE CURL!

Sky looked up.

"That's it," he said.

"Cool," Jordan said. Other kids nodded.

"Yeah," Bastian admitted. "Pretty good."

"That was *great*, Sky," Vicki said softly.

The bell rang: lunch.

12:10 P.M.

———————— Lunch ————————

"Hey, we better go," Vicki said.

"Yeah, but the whole sixth grade will be in the cafeteria," Tim pointed out. "How're we going to keep the teachers from finding out?"

"They'll find out," Jessica predicted. "People will talk."

"Yeah, you, for instance," Bastian muttered.

"*Everybody*, for instance," Jessica retorted. "You think Robert and Corey aren't going to tell Josh?"

The kids all looked at Robert and Corey. The two triplets sat with their brother, Josh, every day at lunch.

"We're innocent!" Robert said, throwing up his arms.

"Yeah!" Corey said. "We didn't do it! We demand to see a lawyer!"

"Listen, guys," Karen said. "We're only trying to do this for one day, right? Six hours. And

70

we're *close*. It'd be a shame to get caught now."

"I say we keep it a class secret," Jasmine said. "I'm not telling anybody. Not even if they torture me."

"It won't work," Sky said quietly. "A story like this is contagious."

Bastian flinched at the word. *Contagious. Quarantine.*

"He's right," Karen said. "Morgan already knows. You really think he can keep quiet about this? No way. And other kids'll find out, too. I say we tell the other sixth graders, *after* we swear them to secrecy. We've got to make them swear they won't tell any teachers until school is over."

"It's worth a try," Jasmine said. "Three o'clock. That's all we're asking. It's less than three hours away."

"Fact," Christopher said.

"Never work," Tim said. "There are about a gazillion teachers' pets in the sixth grade. Maybe more."

Rachel started scribbling a note.

"Wait a sec," Missy said. "Rachel's got something."

"Ah," Bastian muttered. "The Silent Pilot speaks again!"

"This is your last day," Rhonda told him. "Just pretend for one day that you're a nice person."

My dog thinks I'm nice, Bastian thought. He smirked at Rhonda.

Missy took the paper from Rachel and read out loud:

"Maybe the other sixth graders won't tell any teachers if we make them feel included. If they feel like they're part of it."

"Part of it how?" Jasmine asked.

"By keeping the secret," Jessica said, nodding at Rachel. "Then it's like they're sort of getting away with it, too. It's our only hope."

"*Our* only hope?" Jasmine smiled at her. "Sounds like you're with us after all."

"Not really," Jessica said, folding her arms.

* * *

In the cafeteria, Rachel sat with Missy and Rhonda. Miranda Lundstrom, a girl from Mrs. Friedman's class, sat with them.

"Tell me," Miranda begged. "Tell me, tell me, tell me!"

"Swear you won't tell anybody till after school," Missy said.

"I swear, I swear," she said. "Jeez, Missy, what's the big deal?"

"This is really serious," Missy said in a hushed voice. She ripped the wax paper off her sandwich as if she was unwrapping a fabulous gift. "This is Highly Confidential. As in Top Secret."

"All right, already!" Miranda said in an exasperated voice. "I swear! I swear on a stack of pictures of Rob Nelson!"

"That's better!" Missy smiled. Rob Nelson was the cutest boy in the sixth grade. She leaned forward and whispered: "Mr. Fab's out today."

"Yeah?" Miranda said. "You mean out, like: *absent?* Gee, that *is* exciting!"

"We've got no teacher."

"Who's your sub?"

"That's the thing," Missy whispered. *"We don't have one! We're running our own class today!"*

Miranda gave Missy an incredulous look, then glanced over at Rachel. Rachel nodded.

"What?" Miranda hissed. She smacked her forehead.

"Remember," Missy said. "You promised!"

"Who, what–I mean," Miranda sputtered, "how did you get away with that?"

"It started off as a normal day," Missy began.

From the other side of the room Rachel heard a snort of disbelief, a squeal of outraged delight that quickly got squelched. Looking around, Rachel could see dozens of kids in pairs, threes, and fours, heads bent together, all talking intently. She closed her eyes but even so she could feel the story spreading through the cafeteria, carried on thousands of whispered words, a fire burning up a dry forest, jumping from table to table, little flames she could feel licking at her insides. For the second time that day she could feel the pressure of words in her chest, words that wanted to get out but somehow could not come out. She chewed a bite of sandwich and swallowed it down.

12:21 P.M.

——Early Dismissal——

Bastian gulped down lunch. There was a phone right outside the cafeteria. He jammed in the coin and punched in the number to his house.

"I'm sorry," a voice said. "The number you have called—555-7134—has been disconnected. Please—"

He hung up the phone.

Disconnected.

All at once it hit him. He was moving.

Bastian walked down the hallway and out the front door of the school. Nobody tried to stop him. Nobody said *Where-do-you-think-you're-going-young-man?* He couldn't believe how easy it was. He strolled past the flagpole and down the street. The skies had grown heavy with clouds, and the air smelled like rain. He had no idea where he was going and he didn't care. His feet kept moving and he just walked.

He walked past a young woman washing her car. She waved at him and he waved back. In the

74

front yard Bastian saw a little boy playing ball with a bulldog.

Barkley. For the hundredth time that day he tried not to think about the puppy, but not-thinking had turned out to be a lot harder than he'd ever imagined.

He went past a Catholic school, Our Lady of Sorrows, and stopped to watch the kids playing soccer on the playground. They were all wearing uniforms, boys in slacks and white shirts, girls in identical tweed skirts and white blouses. A couple hundred kids and he didn't know a single one of them. He knew that moving to Hawaii would feel exactly like this. No friends. Hundreds of strange kids. Most of them would stay apart, watching, checking him out from a distance.

He would go through his own kind of quarantine.

He left Our Lady of Sorrows and walked to the end of Walden Street. The Galleria mall was down the street to the right, but his feet didn't turn that way. Instead they turned left and began carrying him toward his house. At first going home and seeing Barkley seemed like a terrific idea. But he couldn't do it.

He sailed past his own street, heading straight toward the house of his best friend, John LeClerc. He got to the house and rang the doorbell.

"Yeah?" John's voice came through a crack in the door.

"Hello," Bastian said in his deepest voice. "This is James Warren, the district truant officer. Are you John LeClerc? Open the door! I have a warrant for your arrest! I have a report that you are playing hooky from school today. Don't you realize that's against the law?"

"Bastian!" John laughed and swung open the door; Bastian followed him inside. "You're the last person I expected to see! I thought you were having, like, tons of awesome fun in school. Your *last* day of school."

"John, you won't believe this," Bastian said, following John into the kitchen. "Mr. Fab's out today, right? But they didn't send us a sub! They screwed up in the office, or something. We got no teacher in the class!"

"Yeah, sure," John said. He opened the refrigerator door and looked inside. "And I bet they put free video games in all the classrooms, huh? I don't think so."

"I'm serious! I'm telling you: We've been alone all day! I swear, John! Alone! For a while it looked like Jessica was going to squeal, but she didn't. It's *awesome!*"

"Alone?"

"We're running the class ourselves! We've got a new motto: KIDS RULE!"

John shut the refrigerator.

"I don't believe this!" he said.

"It's wild," Bastian said. "I'm telling you, this

day will go down in history. You've missed a lot of fun, but the day's not over yet. Come to school! Karen's playing Little Miss Teacher. That's why we need you—you've got to help us party!"

"I'm coming!" John yelled. He ran toward his bedroom. "Just let me get my shoes!"

"All right!" Bastian called after him. "This afternoon we're going to crank up the music!"

"Wait!" John said, carrying his shoes into the kitchen. "They won't let me back into school without a note!"

"Don't worry," Bastian said. "You want a note, I'll give you a note. I'll give you a great note. Gimme some paper."

John gave him a sheet of paper and Bastian sat down to write.

"Good thing I've got perfect penmanship," Bastian said as he carefully formed the letters. He laughed. "Yes, sir. You've had a miraculous recovery!"

"C'mon!" John said. "Hurry up!"

12:30 P.M.

——————— Recess ———————

Rachel stood on the playground watching the other kids. She heard a plane in the distance. The air smelled like rain.

She thought of her father.

He was a tall man, all elbows and knees, with dark bushy eyebrows. He'd left home when Rachel was in fourth grade. He and Mom had been arguing, and their fights seemed to grow more ferocious with each new day. Finally Rachel couldn't take it anymore. One day she burst into their bedroom and started shouting at them.

"Stop it! Stop arguing! You should hear yourselves! It's pathetic that two grownups should act the way you do! It's disgusting!"

Dad and Mom looked at her. They looked at each other.

"She's right," Dad said to Mom. The next day he moved out. He moved west. A few months later he bought a small cattle farm in New Mexico. He'd been living there ever since.

She only saw him twice a year now, and there were many days when she missed him terribly: his silly stories, goofy songs, magic tricks that were so amateurish even a baby could figure them out.

The rain smell reminded her of one summer day he took her to a playground. It started pouring rain but they didn't leave. Instead, they stayed on the swings, singing at the top of their lungs while their clothes got soaked.

Why flying? Mr. Snickenberger had asked her. *Why is flying so important to you?*

If I could fly I could see my father whenever I want, she thought. But she never said this, not even to Mom.

She kept replaying the sequence of events: her parents argued, she scolded them, then Dad left. One, two, three. Even now she had the nagging thought that in some way her scolding had been the catalyst for his moving out. Those fights had been horrible, but she wished he was still living at home, arguments or not. She wished she had kept her mouth shut. Back then it had never occurred to her that she had the Right.

The Right to remain silent.

12:50 P.M.

———— Blood ————

After recess Class 6-238 filed back to the room. Rachel walked near the front of the line, right behind Karen and Jasmine.

"Bastian left," Jasmine said. "He just went home."

"I know," Karen said, shrugging.

"His last day of school," Jasmine said. "It's weird to think that we'll never see him again."

Like Tommy Feathers, Rachel thought. It was April 28. The six-month anniversary of Tommy's death. Was she the only one who remembered?

"Bastian's gone!" Tim announced when he walked into the class.

"We know, we know," Jessica sighed.

Just then Jordan came in with Sky, who was limping.

"He's bleeding!" Jordan said. Kids ran over to see. Sure enough, there was a large scrape the size of a half dollar on Sky's knee. A bright rivulet of blood had snaked halfway down his shin. He moved stiffly to his desk and sat down, wincing.

"It's all right," he said.

"Does it hurt?" Karen asked.

Sky nodded and bit his lower lip.

"Sorry about that pass," Jordan said. "Guess I shouldn't have thrown it so low."

"It's not your fault." Sky grimaced.

"That's pretty ugly," Karen said. "You better go down to the nurse."

"I'm okay, really," Sky said.

"He can't go to the nurse!" Tim said.

"Why not?" Jasmine demanded.

"Because he needs a pass," Tim told her. "Who's gonna sign it? Mr. Fab? Our invisible sub? Huh? Are *you* gonna sign it?"

"Hm," Karen said.

"You should just go to her office," Jasmine told Sky. "What's the nurse going to say: 'You can't come in—go bleed somewhere else'?"

"That's what she told me last week," Corey said. "It's a new rule: You can't go to the nurse without a signed pass."

"You better go," Jessica told Sky. "I'll go with you."

"Ooooh," Christopher said, raising his eyebrows and starting to sing: "Sky and Jessica, sittin' in a tree, k-i-s-s—"

"You Neanderthal!" Rhonda said.

"Opinion!" Christopher shouted.

"Shut up!" Jessica pleaded in a whisper.

Rachel nudged Missy. When Missy gave her a questioning look, Rachel nodded and nudged her again.

"Well, it doesn't look that deep," Missy said. "I don't think you need stitches or anything. I can probably take care of it."

"You?" Tim asked skeptically.

"Sure," Missy said. "My father's a doctor. I know something about medicine."

"My father's a heart surgeon but you don't see me going around cutting up people's hearts!" Christopher retorted. He scratched his head. "Though actually that might be kind of fun!"

"This isn't heart surgery," Missy said. "Does Mr. Fab have any Band-Aids or anything?"

She walked to Mr. Fabiano's desk, opened the bottom drawer, and pulled out a first-aid kit.

"Great, this has everything we need."

"Can you really . . . do this?" Sky asked her.

"Sure," Missy said softly. "First we need to wash out the wound. Can you get over to the sink?"

Sky hobbled over. The entire class clustered around him. Rachel stood in back, watching.

"Give him some room to breathe!" Robert said.

"See if you can sort of sit up there," Missy said. "So your knee is right under the faucet."

Sky scooted up onto the counter and pulled his leg around.

"My mother used to give my sister her bath in the sink," Corey said.

"Same with my little brother," Tim said. "Except one time he–"

"Don't say it!" Rhonda begged. "I just ate."

"This is going to hurt a little," Missy said, turning on the water. "You guys, see if you can distract him."

"Try this," Jordan suggested. "Say: 'Peter Piper picked a peck of pickled peppers.'"

"No," Sky said. "Ow!"

"Just a sec," Missy told him.

"Think nice thoughts," Jasmine suggested.

"Yeah, think about surfing," Jordan said.

"Surfing can be pretty dangerous," Sky told them. "A friend of mine got hurt bad his first day surfing on a brand new board."

"Really?"

"He was riding this huge swell, and he wiped out, and his board came shooting up, and caught him right here." Sky pointed at his solar plexus.

"Hey!" Missy said. "You guys are supposed to be distracting him!"

"Ouch!" Sky said.

"Sorry," Missy told him. "That stuff's supposed to kill any infectious germs."

"What happened to your friend?" Tim asked.

"Broke six ribs," Sky said. "He couldn't even move in the water. Luckily, he was able to hold on to his board and float there till somebody swam out to help him."

"There!" Missy said. "Good as new. Well, almost."

They all looked at the bandage. Missy had done a nice, neat job. Sky got off the counter and stood testing his knee.

"Feels pretty good," Sky said. He looked at Missy. "Thanks a lot."

"When you get home, take the bandage off," Missy said. "The air will make it heal faster."

"Not bad," Christopher admitted. "You gonna be a nurse when you grow up?"

"I want to be a doctor," Missy said shyly.

"Haven't you heard?" Jessica asked him. "*Women* can be doctors, too."

"Fact," Rhonda told Christopher.

"Our hero!" Jasmine said, raising Missy's hand in the air.

"It's no big deal," Missy said, though she did look pleased.

"See what I mean?" Tim demanded. He whirled around so Corey and Christopher could slap him five. "KIDS RULE! Who needs the teacher? Who needs the nurse? Huh? Who needs any grownups at all?"

——— Enrichment ———

Rachel stared out the window, looking past the field to the patch of woods beyond. She had heard that deer lived in those woods, and she liked this idea because deer were her favorite animals. A deer knew how to make itself invisible by using camouflage and silence. Deer made no bark, no whinny, no growl, no sound. They were mute.

Or were they? Rachel wondered if silence might be something that deer chose. Maybe they had everybody fooled. Maybe they had invented their own secret language to communicate when nobody was around.

A few large raindrops splattered against the windows. For a minute she sat watching the rain. She guessed that it would be hard to fly a plane in the rain, especially a small plane. (Did planes have windshield wipers, like cars? She should know that, but didn't.) And landing in a rainstorm would be a lot trickier. The rain would cut down visibility.

Rachel looked past Sean O'Day's face to the window where droplets were bouncing off the glass. The rain was starting to fall harder now. She thought of the silent deer getting wet in that patch of woods. Corey jumped up to close the windows.

"Hey, we've got to go to enrichment," Jessica announced.

"Thank you, five-points-below-genius," Tim said.

"Shut up, you troglodyte," Rhonda shot back.

"What's that?" Tim asked.

"Look it up," Rhonda told him smugly.

"Look it up," he mimicked.

Enrichment was the program for gifted students. Early in the school year Rachel had gone to enrichment, too. But when she stopped speaking, Mr. Doblin dropped her from the program.

"I don't want to go to enrichment," Jessica groaned.

"I must go to enrichment," Christopher said. "I must feed my brain! I'm gifted!"

"You've got a gifted belly," Tim said, nodding.

"Shush," Karen said. She looked at Jessica. "You know, I really don't feel like going, either."

"But we have to," Jessica said. "Mr. Doblin will come after us if we don't."

"We're getting all the enrichment you can ask for right here," Karen asked. "Let's skip it today."

"Skip it?" Christopher asked. "How you gonna manage that?"

"Just watch," Karen said, going to the phone behind Mr. Fabiano's desk. She picked it up and dialed a number.

"Order me a pizza while you're at it," Tim suggested.

"Mr. Doblin?" Karen asked. "Hi, this is Karen Ballard in Mr. Fabiano's class. We were wondering if we could maybe miss enrichment today. Yes, sir. We're doing a project here in Mr. Fabiano's class. Sort of like an independent study."

Vicki giggled at that.

"No, sir, Mr. Fabiano is absent today." Karen said again. Pause. "Yes, sir." Another pause. Karen smiled. "Okay, I'll tell them. Thanks, Mr. Doblin."

She hung up the phone.

"That was a close call," she said, grinning. "For a second I thought he wanted to talk to our sub. Anyway, it's all set. We're staying right here."

"Amen," said Jasmine.

"What about me?" Sean asked. "I gotta go to Resource Room. I'm already late."

Everyone turned to look at him.

"Does Mrs. Zemetti really help you?" Robert asked. "I went to her last year. I think she's an alien. Seriously. She's nice but she's from another galaxy."

"Fact," Christopher said. He looked at Sean. "You really have to go?"

Sean shrugged and lowered his eyes. It was no secret that he was a poor reader.

"My dad showed me this trick," Robert told Sean. "For remembering stuff after you read it. I can show you—it's pretty easy."

"So it's decided then," Karen said. "You're staying. We need you right here."

"But what—" Sean said.

"Don't worry," Karen said, getting out of her seat. "I'll arrange everything."

Karen picked up the phone again.

"No answer," she said, frowning.

Just then the door opened and Mrs. Zemetti herself walked into the room. Rachel sat up with a start.

"Come on, Sean," Mrs. Zemetti urged from the doorway. She was the grandmotherly sort of teacher, short and plump, with a pair of thick bifocals around her neck.

"But, um, I gotta do some stuff here," Sean said. He looked confused.

"I'll have you back here in thirty minutes, maybe less," Mrs. Zemetti said with a kind smile. "You'll hardly know you were gone."

Reluctantly, Sean stood. Rachel saw him hesitate by the rain-drenched window, torn between going and trying to stay. She felt sorry for him, but there was nothing she or anyone else could do to help him.

"You are to be commended," Mrs. Zemetti said, smiling at the kids in the classroom. "I can't tell you how nice it is to see a class behaving itself. You can tell that to Mr. Fabiano."

"He's out today," Karen explained as Sean walked to the front of the room. She smiled. "We have a substitute. She just ran to the bathroom."

"Well, please tell her that I said you're a wonderful class," Mrs. Zemetti said.

Mrs. Zemetti and Sean left. For two full seconds the class stayed silent as if holding its collective breath. Then everyone cracked up.

"Shhhh!" Jasmine said but she was laughing, too, bent over.

She opened her eyes wide and, still laughing, pointed at Rachel White. The whole class looked and saw what Jasmine had seen: a small smile on Rachel's face.

1:20 P.M.

D.E.A.R.

"Less than two hours to go!" Jordan said.

Christopher let out a loud whoop.

"You do that again, we'll have fifteen teachers coming through that door," Karen said, pointing. "Is that what you want?"

"Sowwy," Christopher said, pouting and sucking his thumb.

At that moment Bastian and John burst into the room, both wet from the rain.

"Greetings, Earthlings!" John announced with a formal bow. "Take me to your leader! Give me a towel!"

"Yo, John!" Christopher cried. "You finally made it!" He stood and started to applaud.

"I thought you were sick today," Jessica said.

"Feeling much much better!" John said, bowing again. He shook his head, and water from his hair sprayed all over the place.

"Hey, quit that!" Jessica yelled.

"I wrote a note for him," Bastian said. "He skipped *into* school!"

"Yesss!" Christopher sprang up to slap John five.

"You guys smell like wet dogs," Vicki said, wrinkling her nose.

"Thank you, thank you," John said, bowing for the third time. He strolled to the front of the room and fell back into Mr. Fab's empty chair. "I wouldn't miss this for a million bucks!"

John pulled out two bags of candy from his backpack and tossed them to Tim and Christopher.

"Party time!" Christopher cried, ripping open a bag.

"You mean D.E.A.R. time," Karen said, pointing at the board.

John laughed. "You're kidding, right?"

Rachel closed her eyes and pictured Tommy Feathers during D.E.A.R., reading with his face close to the book. He always hummed while he read, and he always hummed the same tune: the *1812 Overture.*

"No way!" Bastian said hotly. "I'm not gonna do D.E.A.R. or D.A.R.E. or D.W.E.E.B. or any other stupid thing! We shouldn't be doing *any* work— we've got no teacher! At this rate we're going to get into the *Guinness Book of World Wimps!*"

"Mr. Fabiano always does D.E.A.R. after lunch," Karen said, as if that settled it.

"Now hear this, now hear this," Bastian said. He cupped his hands around his mouth and spoke as if through a megaphone. "I HAVE AN IMPORTANT ANNOUNCEMENT TO MAKE. MR. FAB IS NOT HERE. REPEAT. MR. FAB IS NOT HERE."

"That's what you think," Tim muttered.

"*I'm* reading," Jessica said.

"Why?" Bastian demanded.

"Because I happen to enjoy it," she replied calmly.

"Yeah, me too," Vicki put in. Some of the girls started pulling out their books.

"Look at this," John said, stuffing two pieces of bubble gum into his mouth. He held up a computer disk. "Anybody up for playing a little DOOM III?"

"Yeah, I do! I'm playing! Lemme go first!"

Tim, Christopher, Robert, Corey, Jordan, Sky, Bastian, and John all rushed to the back of the room and crowded around the computer.

"You guys are so wicked awesome cool!" Rhonda said.

"Fact," Christopher said.

"Go back to D.E.A.R.," Tim told Rhonda.

"Shut up," Rhonda told him.

"I feel sorry for you," Tim said. "I really do."

That's how D.E.A.R. time went. The boys played DOOM III; the girls read. Rachel looked over at Sean's empty desk. She wondered which one he would choose—the computer game, probably, even though he didn't usually hang out with the other boys much. The room felt different, emptier, now that he was gone.

Rachel pulled out her book. She loved reading, but the whole idea of D.E.A.R. bugged her. Why cram reading into a fifteen-minute time block and give it a cutesy name like that? Why not just call it *reading?* It was the world's dumbest title—you didn't drop everything when you read, you picked something up!

Still, reading was the best part of the afternoon, especially on a rainy day like this. There was a cozy feeling in the room when the whole class, including Mr. Fabiano, read their books together.

Rachel picked up her book, *A Beginner's Flight Manual.* It was the most detailed book she had ever read on how to become a pilot. She read slowly so she wouldn't miss a single word:

Several steps are involved in earning a pilot's license. Each one requires many hours of practice. The next three chapters will cover the following areas:

Chapter 8: Simulated Solo. Engineers have designed machines known as "flight simulators" to help train pilots. These machines are totally realistic, with all the pedals, instruments, rudders, and throttles you have in a plane. Sitting in a simulator on the ground feels like you're actually flying in a jet or propeller airplane. A simulator allows you to experience flight conditions—takeoff, flight, approach, and landing—in a controlled setting where you can't get hurt.

Chapter 9: Supervised Solo. This happens much later in your training. In this step you can actually fly the plane under the guidance and strict supervision of an experienced pilot. Often the pilot will take off or land the plane but allow you to fly for short periods of time.

Rachel looked up from her book; the room had begun to turn bright. She looked out the window and saw that the rain had stopped and the sunlight was playing sparkling tricks on the new grass.

For some reason this sudden light reminded Rachel of her first airplane flight. She was ten years old, flying to visit her father in New Mexico. The plane left in a heavy rainstorm, rose through thick clouds, and then burst through into the purest sunlight, the bluest skies Rachel had ever seen.

Chapter 10: Solo Flight. This is the ultimate goal: to fly on your own.

Exploration

"Okay, guys, we better stop," Karen said.

"No!" Christopher cried from the computer. "I'm just about to kill this guy!"

"We've got Exploration," Karen said, pointing at the schedule.

Tim and Jordan booed softly. Christopher began sounding a low chant: "Bo-ring . . . Bo-ring . . ."

Rachel sighed and slowly closed her book. As far as she could tell, "Exploration" was just a snazzy word for geography, which boiled down to old-fashioned map skills. She dreaded this subject, and she suspected that Mr. Fabiano felt the same way since he scheduled it so late in the day. Not even a teacher like Mr. Fabiano could breathe much life into map reading, though he certainly tried to show his students how important it was.

If you want to fly you have to know how to read a map, Mr. Fabiano told her one time. *Lon-*

gitude and latitude. Elevation. There's no way around it. If you want to be a pilot you have to know this stuff cold.

But it's so deadly dull, she had written on a slip of paper.

"Don't even think about it," Tim said, shaking his head. "We're not doing any more work!"

"This won't take long," Karen said. She started passing around the photocopies. "There's just one worksheet, and then we're home free. I bet we can knock it off in twenty minutes. Where's the legend?"

"Right over there," John said, pointing at Bastian.

"Very funny."

"It's true," John said smugly. "He's the legend because this is his last day of school."

"I'm gone," Bastian said. "I'm history. Have a nice life."

"Waahh!" Christopher cried, furiously rubbing both eyes.

"Good-bye," Jasmine said coldly. "Now where's the map legend?"

"Do I have to spell it out for you guys?" John asked, pointing at Bastian. "It's his last day. We have to do a rock ritual."

"It's not on the schedule," Karen said doubtfully.

"Forget the freakin' schedule!" John cried. "He's leaving! This is our last chance!"

"Fact," Christopher put in.

For a second nobody spoke.

"I guess you're right," Karen said reluctantly. "Mr. Fab probably would've put it on the schedule if he'd known it was his last day."

"It just seems weird to do it without Mr. Fab," Jessica said.

"Map skills or rock ritual?" Missy asked. "Which way should we go? Should we vote?"

"What do *you* think, Bastian?" Vicki asked.

Bastian was looking out the window.

"He's thinking about Hawaii and all those hula hula girls," Tim said.

"You bet," Bastian said. He was really thinking about Barkley, flying alone across the Pacific, the largest ocean on earth. The flight would leave tonight at 6 P.M.

"Okay, who votes for a rock ritual?" Karen said.

Everybody raised his or her hand except Jasmine and Jessica.

"Opposed?" Karen asked. The class stared at the two girls but they still didn't raise their hands.

"Are you waiting for a third choice?" Christopher asked.

"I abstain," Jessica said, arms folded.

"Me, too," Jasmine put in.

"Oh, brother!" Tim grabbed his head.

"C'mon, we're running out of time," Karen said. "Go get the rocks, Bastian."

1:40 P.M.

———Rock Ritual———

Bastian went to the closet. From the top shelf he took down a large wooden bowl. Inside there were about a dozen beautiful rocks: polished agates and geodes, glittering chunks of pyrite, and several quartz crystals. The bowl was heavy, and he had to balance it carefully so it wouldn't drop. He put the bowl in the middle of the circle.

Mr. Fabiano was big on rituals, especially inventing new rituals for things that mattered. He had a special welcome ritual for when a new kid came into the class. He had the ritual of playing music during writing time. He had the ritual of reading aloud a certain book, *The Day You Were Born*, whenever someone had a birthday.

The purpose of the rock ritual was to say goodbye to a class member who was leaving. Mr. Fabiano called it a "closure ritual." The class made a circle around the person and watched while that person chose one of the rocks. Everybody else took turns holding the rock while sharing a memory about the person who was leaving. The rock got passed around the circle from student to student, soaking up memory after memory, story after story. The departing person took the rock away when he or she left.

Rachel remembered the rock ritual they had when Miss Wilcox, their student teacher, left the class in February. In October they had tried to do a rock ritual after Tommy Feathers died, but that time it didn't work. They used the pyrite cube–"fool's gold"–that had been Tommy's favorite rock. The pyrite cube got passed from student to student but nobody had anything to say. Now the golden cube was sitting on Mr. Fabiano's desk.

"Ah, the ritual of the sacred rocks!" Christopher exclaimed, bowing so low his head touched the floor.

"For once, act your age and not your IQ," Jessica suggested. Some kids laughed at that.

"Gee, the last time I heard that one I fell off my pet dinosaur!" Christopher exclaimed.

"Shush," Karen urged.

The class waited while Bastian peered into the bowl and picked up a fist-sized rock, brown on one side, studded with sharp white crystals on the other. He moved the rock into a shaft of sunlight and the crystals threw tiny rainbows onto the wall.

Karen clapped twice.

"The ritual of the rock begins in silence," she said.

Bastian put the rock in front of him and everyone closed their eyes for one minute of silence.

Bastian closed his eyes. He felt the strangest feeling inside him, a sensation that had been growing during the day: a jagged kind of sadness he had never felt before. He opened his eyes and peeked at the other kids. He had spent eight months with them. He would try to keep in touch with a friend like John, but the rest of them would drift out of his life forever. He didn't feel broken up about leaving any of them. So why this sadness so sharp, so sudden? It didn't make sense.

Sean O'Day came and squeezed into the circle next to Rachel. At that instant all Rachel could think of was Tommy Feathers, the way he always scurried to sit next to her during circle time.

That was the thing about Tommy. She might forget his dirty hands, or the off-key way he hummed during writing time. But she would never, ever forget the way he looked at her. A look filled with love that was transparent as the cleanest glass. You could see right through it. Would anyone else ever love her like that?

"All right," Karen said. She picked up the rock Bastian had chosen and handed it to Christopher.

"My turn? Okay, well, I remember the time

last fall we were playing kickball. We were losing, like, nine to nothing. We scored a bunch of runs in the last inning. And you kicked a grand slam to win it, ten-nine."

"Yeah." Bastian nodded. "And Rick Frost tried to trip me when I came around third. Dork!"

Christopher passed the rock to Robert.

"I remember at the beginning of the year when you made that substitute cry," Robert said.

"Yess!" Christopher said, raising his fist. Tim and John gave each other high fives.

"Remember when you whipped those pennies against the blinds?" Robert asked. "That was so loud!"

Rachel remembered. The substitute teacher was an older woman who couldn't control the class. Kids threw airplanes, spitballs, Cheez Doodles. She demanded to know who threw the pennies at the blinds and when nobody would tell her, she started to cry.

"That was so excellent!" Christopher said.

"That was so mean," Jasmine muttered.

Robert passed the rock to Corey. He examined it, then looked up and grinned.

"Remember when you blew up that mailbox?" he said.

"I was there!" John said, drumming his thighs. "Ooooh! That was great!"

"Who, me?" Bastian asked innocently.

"He put a cherry bomb in, shut the door, and

BLAM!" Corey said. "There was metal all over the place."

"Thank you, thank you," Bastian said, nodding left and right.

"Whose house was it?" Vicki asked.

"Who cares?" Christopher said. Corey passed the rock to Sean.

Sean took the rock and slowly turned it over in his hands.

"Well, I remember your birthday party," he said softly.

"We threw Mr. Fab into the pool!"

Everybody smiled.

"Yeah," Jasmine said, "and your mother ironed all his paper money to dry it. Remember that?"

"He wasn't even mad," Tim said. "My old man would kill me if we threw him into the pool."

"Shh," Karen said. "It's Sean's turn."

"You got that puppy for your birthday," Sean said. "That's the kind of dog I want to get. I'm saving my money."

"Yeah," Bastian said. And he felt it again. A rush of sadness—strange, mysterious—welling up inside him. And all at once he got it. He understood. He had been moving toward it all day, but he hadn't figured it out until that very moment.

The sadness was about Barkley.

Dad was right. It would be flat-out wrong to put Barkley through the Quarantine. Four months was one hundred and twenty-two days. Two thousand nine hundred and twenty-eight hours. One hundred and seventy-five thousand six hundred and eighty minutes. That was too long for a little puppy to wait, no matter how many times Bastian visited him. It would be cruel to put Barkley through all that.

A moral decision. And he knew the right thing to do.

He had to give Barkley away.

Give Barkley away?

Yes.

No decision had ever felt more right. Or made him feel more miserable.

Now he understood the real reason for this rock ritual. It was a closure ritual. A chance to say goodbye, not to the other kids, but to Barkley. He tried out the words, saying them under his breath.

Goodbye, Barkley.

Sean passed the rock to Rachel.

"You gonna pass?" asked Tim, nervously bouncing his knee up and down.

Rachel held the rock in one hand, a pen in the other. At the far end of the room she could see the picture of Tommy Feathers.

According to his parents, Tommy Feathers went to bed at a normal time and never woke up. Dr. Norton was preparing an autopsy, but he said that preliminary indications were that the boy had died from natural causes.

Rachel swallowed and stared at the picture. Whenever she looked at it she imagined that he was looking for her.

Natural causes. Tommy had been fourteen years old when he died. How natural was that?

"You passing, or what?" Tim asked again. "C'mon, give it here."

Rachel gave Bastian a level look. Then she leaned forward and began to scribble on a note card.

"We'll be here all day!" Tim muttered.

Rachel handed the card to Missy. She read it and blew out her fat cheeks.

"You want me to read this?" Missy asked. Rachel nodded. Missy read the card in a clear voice:

I remember how you teased Tommy Feathers.

Silence. Kids glanced from Rachel to Bastian.

"Yeah, so?" Bastian said. "Big deal."

"Aren't we supposed to tell, like, good memories?" Jasmine asked.

"A memory is a memory," Missy said.

Rachel bent and started to write on the other side of her card.

"She had her turn," Tim said. "C'mon, pass the freakin' rock!"

"Yeah!" Christopher said, but everybody waited for Rachel to finish writing.

You raced him to the bus, Missy read in an angry voice, *but as soon as he started running you'd stop and let him keep going all the way to the bus. He was a slow kid and you teased him. You called him Doctor Drool.*

"So what?" Bastian said, shrugging. "Is it my fault the kid drooled? Yeah, I teased him. I tease everybody. Name one person in here I *don't* tease, huh?"

Nobody spoke.

"What?" Bastian shouted, looking around at the other kids. "You think I was the only one, huh?"

"Shush!" Karen said.

"Hey, I didn't kill him!" Bastian hissed. His eyes narrowed. His voice got low and gravelly. "The kid had medical problems, okay? He died in his sleep! And he was a pain in the butt! Everybody's afraid to say it, but it's true! You know it and I know it!"

Rachel was writing again, lips compressed with fury.

"I think we should stop—" Jessica began.

"Yeah, maybe we'd better—"

"You should talk!" Bastian shouted at Rachel. "Why don't you write about the fifty million hearts and valentines he made you!"

"Will you please keep it down!" Karen begged, but Bastian ignored her.

"Remember that time he asked you to be his girlfriend?" he yelled at Rachel. "You blew him off! You just laughed at him! SHUT UP, RACHEL! JUST SHUT UP!"

He grabbed the pen out of Rachel's hand and threw it across the room. Rachel balled up the note and threw it at Bastian. It bounced off his chest. Then she dropped her face into her hands and started sobbing. Her shoulders shook. The sobs filled the room and they startled the class because they carried the buried sound of a voice they had not heard for half a year.

"It's okay," Sean whispered, putting his hand on her shoulder. With his other hand he picked up the note and unwrapped it.

Remember that little Nerf football you gave him for his birthday? Sean read quietly. *Tommy kept it in his desk. He told me it was the best present he ever got. He looked up to you, Bastian. He trusted you.*

Bastian closed his eyes. There, in the darkness, he saw the whole thing: Barkley, Tommy, the Nerf football. Barkley and Tommy looking at him.

Bastian leaned forward and started to cry.

Everybody froze.

Suddenly Bastian sprang up. He drew back his arm and threw the rock at the window. By some miracle it flew through a four-inch space between the opened top window and the glass below it. Bastian swore and ran out of the room. John ran out after him.

—— Tommy Feathers ——

Class 6-238 stayed in the circle. The room was silent.

"I told you it was dangerous to run a class without a teacher," Jessica said. "You guys thought I was crazy but I was right: People can get hurt. When I said that I didn't just mean physically hurt. I meant–"

"Two points for Jessica," Christopher mocked.

"Well, this is what I was talking about!" she retorted. "Kids aren't equipped to handle stuff like this! Look at Bastian."

"He had it coming," Rhonda said.

"Shut up!" Tim told her.

"Hey, everybody take it easy," Vicki said. "That's over with."

"Look, it's not the end of the world," Karen said. "A kid in our class died and some people cried. What's so horrible about that?"

"Today's the six-month anniversary," Missy

said in a soft voice. "Tommy died on October twenty-eighth."

Everybody looked at the calendar. Rachel sat up. She took a tissue and blew her nose.

"I always thought it was weird," Missy said.

"What?"

"That we stopped talking about him," Missy said. "I mean, first he was here, then he was gone, and we just . . . "

"What did you expect?" Tim asked.

"I don't know," Missy said, shrugging her big shoulders. "That we'd at least mention him once in a while."

Rachel wiped her eyes. She took a deep quavery breath and the class turned to her as if she might speak, but she did not.

"It's true," Vicki said. "We never talk about him."

"I think about him a lot," Robert said.

"Yeah, me too," Corey said. "I've had dreams about Tommy."

"We never wrote about him," Jasmine said.

"Fact," Christopher said. He nodded.

"Let's write, right now," Karen said. "C'mon, let's do it."

"No way," Tim said. He sat on his hand. "Uh uh. I'm finished writing. I've got writer's cramp."

"C'mon," Karen urged. "We've got just enough time before the assembly."

"What I want to know is: Who made you the teacher?" Tim demanded.

"You got a better idea?" Karen asked him.

Everybody got up and walked back to their desks. Rachel went to the stereo. She flipped through the CDs until she found what she was looking for–the *1812 Overture*.

The music began, lively, stirring. As much as anything those notes brought the presence of Tommy Feathers back into class. Rachel had finally gotten her eyes dry, but now the tears started coming back and she went to fetch the box of tissues.

Missy

Yes, he was a little weird. But he was the sweetest thing. He adored Rachel. He'd look at her with those big puppy dog eyes. And he was so nice to me. He was mostly nice to everyone. And he was an amazing cook. I guess it runs in the family. He used to bring lots of stuff from Feathers' Bakery into class. It was not good stuff if you were trying to lose weight but it was always delicious. My personal favorites were the lemon doughnuts. Just before he died he brought in raspberry pie, pieces for everybody in the class. I guess that was his goodbye gift to us. He made a whole pie out of golden raspberries and gave it to Rachel. *Golden raspberries!* I mean, who ever heard of golden raspberries?

Tim

He had a big head. It sounds freaky to say that about him, but that's the thing I remember most. I remember last year when we went to an assembly for bike safety. We were all trying on helmets but for Tommy they had to find one that was adult size–extra large. That big head made him look a little freaky. The first time my little brother met him, he stared and I had to tell him to quit it. But it was pretty freaky seeing a kid with a head that big.

Jasmine

Last fall Mr. Fab said–not all stories have happy endings. Boy, that's for sure.

I'll never forget seeing him at Feathers' Bakery–his parents really loved him. You could just tell. They didn't care that he was a little slow–and they didn't treat him any different than anyone else. He waited on customers, boxed doughnuts, poured coffee, counted out change. They got up at 5 A.M. on weekend mornings to make doughnuts, and Tommy got up with them–Mom said they were trying to make him independent, so he could run the bakery himself someday.

Just before Christmas I went into Feathers' Bakery to get some jelly rolls. Mr. and Mrs. Feathers looked so sad. They didn't smile–they hardly said a thing. It was the saddest thing–their only son, dead. I haven't been able to go back there ever since.

Christopher

Fact: Tommy Feathers died on October 28th. Fact: My father has had at least a dozen patients die in the operating room during heart surgery. Fact: Everyone dies. It's sad, but it happens.

Opinion: As soon as Tommy Feathers died people stopped telling the truth about him. Fact: He was a pretty good cook but his hands were never that clean. Fact: I've seen Tommy Feathers push down younger kids and make them cry. Fact: I've heard him tell dirty jokes. Nasty jokes. Opinion: Tommy Feathers was not the nicest person in the world. I'm not saying he was evil, I'm just saying he had plenty of faults like everyone else. Why should we turn him into some kind of saint just because he died?

Rachel

Dear Bastian,

I'm sorry about what happened today. It's true I was mad at you because you teased Tommy. I wish I could pretend that you were the only one who did that, but you weren't. You're right: Lots of kids teased him, in little ways or big. I was mean to him, too. I guess getting mad at you was easier than facing up to what I did. He used to send me little valentines during class. I'd roll my eyes, or make a face at Missy. That would make Tommy so sad. I wonder if I'll ever forgive myself for that.

You weren't always mean to him. I remember the time Tommy hit a home run in kickball. You and Tim picked him up and carried him around the field on your shoulders. You couldn't see his face because you were carrying him but he was just beaming. You made him a hero that day. I'll never forget that.

Sorry you got upset. I'd hate this to be the last thing you remember about this school.

Sincerely,
Rachel

The door opened. Bastian and John walked into the room. Some of the kids turned to look at Bastian.

"What're you staring at?" John demanded.

Without looking at anybody Bastian walked over to his desk, took out a piece of paper, and started to write.

Rachel brought her paper to Bastian and laid it on his desk. When Bastian ignored her and continued writing, she turned and went back to her seat.

"MAY I HAVE YOUR ATTENTION," Mr. Peacock said over the loudspeaker. "ALL SIXTH

GRADE CLASSES SHOULD PROCEED IMME-
DIATELY TO THE AUDITORIUM FOR THE
ASSEMBLY."

"Okay, we better line up," Jasmine said, taking a deep breath.

"Assembly," Tim muttered. "Who are we
going to see?"

"Some kind of storyteller," Karen said. "His
name is Klof Selat. I think he's Hungarian."

"What kind of twisted name is that?" Christopher asked. He went over to Robert and made
his eyes squinty. "Hi, my name is Klof Selat. How
do you do?"

"This is it, guys!" Karen said. "Once we get
into the auditorium we're home free. Let's keep
those lines straight!"

"But not too straight," Jasmine put in.

"C'mon!" John said to Bastian.

"Go on ahead," Bastian said, writing furiously.
"I'll catch up."

"Are you okay?" Missy whispered to Rachel.
Rachel nodded. As she left the classroom, Sean
came up to her.

"I was wondering . . ." he said. "Can I walk you
home today?"

Rachel raised her eyes to smile at him. She
had not said a word, but the smile was as good
as a word because it clearly said: "Yes."

2:25 P.M.

—— School Assembly ——

Bastian ran out of the classroom and sprinted down the hallway until he caught up to the rest of the class. From the back of the line he watched the other kids walking ahead of him. The girls walked first, Karen and Jasmine with Jessica a half-step behind. Rhonda came next, followed by Vicki, Missy, and Rachel. Sean walked behind Rachel. After a short gap Christopher came ambling along, followed by Corey and Robert, then Sky, Jordan, Tim, and John.

"Here," Bastian said to John. He handed him a slip of paper. "Can you give this to Mr. Fabiano on Monday?"

"Piece o' cake," John said, nodding. "Piece o' crumb cake."

"I mean it," Bastian said. "It's important. Don't forget."

"Hey, don't worry," John said. "I won't."

Last day of school. And there was one last

114

thing Bastian had to do before the day was over.

"Wait here," he told John. Bastian picked up his pace until he was walking beside Sean O'Day.

"Hi," Bastian said.

Sean looked over, surprised. They hardly ever spoke to each other.

"I need someone to take care of my puppy," Bastian said. "I'm not bringing him to Hawaii."

"Why not?" Sean asked.

"It's a long story. You want him?"

"What?" Sean wasn't sure he had heard right.

"I asked if you want my dog," Bastian said.

"You're giving me your puppy?"

"Yeah," Bastian said. "You said you've been wanting to get a dog, right? Well, you want him or not?"

"Well, yeah," Sean said. He still couldn't believe what he was hearing.

"Okay, he's yours," Bastian said. "But if I ever hear you're not taking care of him, I'll come back here and rip both your arms off. Okay?"

Sean nodded seriously.

"I mean that," Bastian said. His eyes had teared up again.

"You don't have to worry," Sean told him.

"You need to come over my house after school."

Rachel walked down a hallway that was long and smooth as an airport runway. She thought of Amelia Earhart, tired and hungry near the end of her first solo trip across the Atlantic, trying to find a place to land her plane. *It's not about breaking any record,* Rachel thought. *It's about finding a place to land, a way to land, so nobody gets hurt.*

Class 6-238 was jumpy with adrenaline. It made them walk faster than usual, so fast that when they got to the auditorium they almost ran smack into the back of Mrs. Kiefer's class ahead of them.

Rachel walked into the auditorium. The enormous room teemed with talking kids. She experienced the sound as an ocean, rolling, shifting, sighing. As Class 6-238 took their seats, a little ripple of excitement flickered through one side of the auditorium. Other sixth graders looked over, winking, giving them the thumbs-up sign, clapping softly.

"We're famous!" Rhonda whispered as she took her seat next to Rachel.

"Act normal," Karen reminded everyone.

Down by the stage Mr. Peacock was talking to a tall, strange man. Rachel guessed that was Klof Selat, the storyteller. Next to him there was a woman with a fancy camera around her neck.

"She must be from the newspaper," Missy whispered to Rachel.

"Everyone please take your seats," Mr. Peacock said. He stood at the microphone, waiting until all the talking had stopped.

"This is a very special day," Mr. Peacock said

to the hushed crowd. "We are all in for a real treat this afternoon. We have a wonderful storyteller with us, a man who comes all the way from Hungary, in Eastern Europe. I know you will give our guest your complete attention. It is my pleasure to introduce to you Klof Selat!"

Applause. Rachel studied the man as he moved to the microphone. He had a beard and long ponytail. More than anything, he reminded her of Paul Bunyan.

"I've got a story to tell you," he began in a voice so amazingly low it was practically gravel. He paused and looked around fiercely, as if daring anyone to disagree. "But I'm going to need some help for this one. I'll need four teachers."

At this Mr. Peacock sprang to the microphone.

"Why don't we have the sixth-grade teachers come up here," he suggested. There was more applause as Mrs. Reilly, Mrs. Friedman, and Mrs. Kiefer made their way to the front of the auditorium. They stood smiling nervously in front of the storyteller.

"Oh, no!" Missy whispered.

Rachel squeezed her armrest, hard.

"Mr. Fabiano isn't here," Mr. Peacock said, searching the crowd. His eyes fixed on Karen Ballard. "Karen, who is your substitute?"

Karen stood. Six hundred and eleven kids, thirty-one teachers, one storyteller, one newspaper photographer, and one principal stared at her. Rachel could see that Karen's hands were shaking. *If anybody can handle a moment like this,* she thought, *it's Karen Ballard.*

Karen hesitated, biting her lip.

"Who is your substitute?" Mr. Peacock asked again.

Karen hesitated a second, then threw up her arms. It was the only time Rachel had seen Karen make such a gesture, and it was so helpless, so completely out of character, Rachel almost burst out laughing.

"Well?" Mr. Peacock demanded. He leaned forward to listen.

"Well, um, see . . ." Karen stammered. "See, we didn't have a sub today. We didn't have anybody."

At that moment the photographer swiveled around, her flash went off, and all hell broke loose.

Sunday, April 30

9:04 P.M.

−Karen Ballard's House −

Karen lay in bed with her eyes closed. She was tired of talking. And arguing. Her parents were furious on Friday, angry with her on Saturday, and they were still pretty mad on Sunday. She couldn't remember the last time they had been so mad for so long.

All weekend Karen had listened to them. *We are disappointed in you. Your mother and I expect you to show better judgment than that.*

When it was Karen's turn to speak, she had repeated eleven words over and over and over until they began to lose their meaning: *We ran the class, we did our work, we behaved ourselves.*

Character, her mother reminded her, *is how you act when no one is watching.*

I know, Karen said stubbornly. *I'm proud of how we acted.*

This was true, mostly. Except for one small thing, her conscience was clear. On Friday when

Mrs. Zemetti came into the room to get Sean O'Day, Karen had said that the sub had gone to the bathroom. That was a lie, a small lie, but it was still wrong, and she intended to apologize to Mrs. Zemetti.

The downstairs phone started ringing. It hadn't stopped ringing all weekend. She hoped that it wasn't for her, but in a moment she heard footsteps on the stairs. The door opened and the silhouette of her mother appeared in the doorway.

"Karen, are you awake?" her mother asked. Karen could hear the coldness in her mother's voice. Would her parents stay mad at her forever?

"Yeah."

"Mr. Fabiano is on the phone. He wants to talk to you."

Karen climbed out of bed and stumbled into the hallway. This was the call she'd been dreading.

"Hello?" Karen thought her voice sounded faint, uncertain.

"Hi, Karen. This is Mr. Fabiano." Pause. "I'm really sorry to be calling you so late at night but I just got home."

"That's okay," she said softly. Another pause. "I guess you heard, huh?"

"I just got off the phone with Mr. Peacock," he said. "He's pretty upset."

"I know," Karen said.

"I'm just trying to figure out what happened on Friday," Mr. Fabiano said.

"We ran the class ourselves," she said, flattered that he had called her.

"Yes, Mr. Peacock told me that," Mr. Fabiano said. "But what did you *do* all day?"

"We did our work, mostly," she said.

"You did?"

"Yes, sir. Some kids fooled around a little, but we got a lot of work done, too. I . . . ran the class, sort of, and I followed the plans you left for the sub. Let's see, we did spelling, math, D.E.A.R. We did just about everything."

"Did you write?" he asked.

"Yes, sir. We wrote a ton, as a matter of fact. We wrote, like, four times, I think."

"All right," he said. He sounded relieved. "Karen, did anything out of the ordinary happen? Anything I should know about?"

"Well, yes." Karen took a deep breath. "Bastian told us it was his last day. So we took a vote and decided to have a rock ritual."

"When was that?" Mr. Fabiano asked.

"Around two o'clock," she said. "Before the assembly. We passed around the rock but when it was Rachel's turn she started writing Bastian these notes. About Tommy Feathers. He started yelling at her. They got into this really big argument."

"About Tommy?"

"Yes, sir," Karen said. She swallowed. "It ended up okay, but it got a little scary for a while. They were both crying."

"Did Rachel . . . talk?" he asked.

"No," Karen said. "But she cried a lot. Bastian did, too."

"I see."

Another pause.

"Mr. Fabiano, in a way I feel like I should apologize. But in another way I don't. It's kind of hard to explain."

"Karen, we'll talk about this tomorrow."

"Mr. Fab? Are you mad at me?"

"Should I be?" he asked.

"No, I don't think so," Karen replied. "I really don't."

"I'll see you tomorrow morning," he told her. "Get some sleep."

Monday, May 1

Room 238

Mr. Fabiano stood staring at his students. Rachel had never seen his face so somber. He hadn't spoken once since she and her classmates filed into the room and quietly took their seats. Now they sat at their desks, looking at him. And he stared back.

Rachel glanced around the classroom. She noticed that Sean was wearing what looked like a clean T-shirt. He looked over and flashed her a big smile.

"GOOD MORNING," Mr. Peacock said over the loudspeaker. The class sat in silence while the principal made the announcements. Mr. Peacock made no mention of the parents, reporters, and TV cameras stationed in front of the school.

Everyone stood for the Pledge of Allegiance. Rachel heard Mr. Fabiano's voice. *With liberty. And justice. For all.*

"Attendance," Mr. Fabiano said. "Karen?"

"Here."

"Rhonda?"

"Here."

"Christopher?"

"Present." He smirked.

"Is something funny, Christopher?" Mr. Fabiano asked, looking up from his sheet. "Something we all should know about?"

"No, sir," Christopher replied quietly.

Pause. Mr. Fabiano glanced down at the attendance sheet.

"Bastian . . . ? Oh yes, he moved." He wrote something on the sheet. "Tim?"

"Here."

"Robert? Corey?"

"We're here."

"Melinda?"

"Here."

"Jessica?"

"Here."

"Rachel?" He glanced up and marked her as present.

"I'm here," she said quietly.

Everyone turned. Rachel blushed and low-ered her eyes. She felt a little silly. Mr. Fabiano stood up.

"You spoke!"

"Yes," she said. She glanced over at Missy, who looked as if she had seen a ghost. The expression of shock softened into a grin.

"Hi Rachel!" Missy whispered.

"Hi," Rachel said.

"It is so good to hear your voice," Mr. Fabiano said, smiling.

She looked up for a few seconds before realiz-ing he was waiting for her to say something more.

"I know," she said at last.

"A time to keep silence and a time to speak," Mr. Fabiano said. "To every thing there is a sea-son." He nodded. "That's from the Bible."

"I know," she said again, and kids laughed, as if now those were the only two words she could say.

"It seems that we have lots to talk about," Mr. Fabiano said to the class. He spoke in a calm voice. "I wasn't here on Friday. But it has come to my attention that Friday was not your typical day. Something happened, right here in this classroom. Something unusual. Something seri-ous. And I would like to know about it."

He got up and walked slowly toward the back

of the room. At Tommy Feathers's empty desk he stopped and sat down. Kids swiveled around to look at him.

"I want you to write me a letter," he said. "What I want to know is this: What happened? Nobody has a monopoly on the truth. Each of you will have your version."

He pointed at a sign on one of the walls.

CHARACTER IS HOW YOU ACT WHEN NOBODY'S WATCHING.

"You've read this sign a hundred times, right? All right, then. How did *you* act when no teacher was watching? Write. Don't just give me a bunch of fluff. Dig under the surface. Tell me something I don't know. Don't rush. See how much you can get down in twenty minutes. Then we'll get together and share."

Jasmine

Dear Mr. Fabiano,

At first it was sort of a prank—no more teachers, no more books, yuk yuk yuk. But after a while we started feeling kinda proud of what we were doing. Sort of like: "We don't need any grownups—we can do it ourselves!"

What I can't get my parents to understand is how totally *normal* the day was. We worked,

130

talked, voted on decisions. True, some kids were talking out more, and making wisecracks, but most of the time we felt pretty close. And there were a couple of times I felt like we (the class) were a team—a real family.

Your student,
Jasmine

Jessica

Dear Mr. Fab,

I DO NOT, REPEAT, DO NOT want to write about Friday! I'm sorry but I'm sick of talking about it! This is the LAST TIME I'll let anyone talk me into a stunt like that. Boy, did I get in trouble with my parents, especially my father! Here's a sample of my weekend:

Dad: Didn't you know it was wrong, Jessica?

Me: Yes.

Dad: Didn't you know it was dangerous for a bunch of kids to be unsupervised all day?

Me: Yes, sort of.

Dad: Sort of?

Me: Well, yes.

Dad: Then why did you do it?

Mom: Stop it! You're putting her on trial!

Dad: I'm just trying to get at the truth!

Mom: You're cross-examining her!

I NEVER want to go through a weekend like that. And to think that I was the only kid who voted AGAINST the idea of us running the class in the first place!!!!

Super-Annoyed,
Jessica

Christopher

Dear Mr. Fab,

Saturday morning the phone rang. It was a reporter from the *National Enquirer!* I think he was calling my mother, because she's president of the P.T.A., but he seemed happy to talk to me.

"We heard that some strange things happened in your class on Friday. Satanic rituals, that sort of thing. Is that true?"

I told him: "We got out the Ouija board and used it to try to contact the spirit of Tommy Feathers, a kid in our class who died in October."

The man asked: "Really?"

I told him: "No, I'm kidding. We did our work, read, wrote. It was just like any other day."

He seemed disappointed, and hung up.

Here's the saddest fact of all: *Nothing happened.* Don't worry about whether or not we were good. Believe me, we were *too* good. No rock music, no party, no nothing. For about twenty minutes some of us played a computer game. Big deal!

Pathetically,
Christopher

Missy

Dear Mr. Fabiano,

Friday was an important day. We proved that kids could have fun and still act a lot more responsibly than most grownups (like my parents) ever thought we could.

Did we do the right thing? Tough question. In the Revolutionary War the colonists dumped tea into Boston Harbor. Was that wrong? My mother thinks that's not a fair comparison, but I disagree. We saw the chance for more freedom. We took that chance. And we were willing to pay the price.

Sincerely,
Missy

P.S. Did you see the photograph of our class in the newspaper? That's the best picture of me I've ever had taken!

Karen

Dear Mr. Fab,

You've been telling me all year that I'm a leader but I don't think I realized it until Friday. It was me who went to the office and decided not to tell Mrs. Pierce that they forgot to send us a sub. It was me who gave the class the idea in the first place. I talked the other kids into it. I take full responsibility for what happened.

I went to the office to tell them that we had no teacher. But when I got there I realized that all they would do is send us some stranger to tell us what we were supposed to do. Who needed that? We *knew* what to do. I figured: Hey, we can run the class ourselves.

Jessica thought it was really dangerous for us to be without a teacher. My parents say the same thing. I thought and thought about it all weekend and I still respectfully disagree. We handled every problem that came up until the rock ritual when Rachel and Bastian got into that awful argument. I'll admit it: That was very, very scary. That was the only time I wished you were with us. But then again, if you were with us I seriously doubt we ever would have talked and written about Tommy Feathers.

Sincerely,
Karen Ballard

Bastian

Today is Friday. (You won't read this till Monday.) Today has been BASTIAN'S TERRIBLE HORRIBLE NO GOOD DAY.

We just did a rock ritual. (This is my last day in class.) Rachel accused me of picking on Tommy Feathers. She's right. But it was nothing against him. That's my style. I picked on lots of kids when I moved here, and I'll probably do the same thing in Hawaii. It's like what they say in the Air Force: "The best defense is a good offense."

Today I cried in school. I haven't done that since first grade! Kids probably think I got upset because of what Rachel said. Wrong! It was because of Barkley, my puppy. I can't take him to Hawaii. It's too cruel to quarantine him for so long, so after school I'm going to give him to Sean O'Day. It's the best thing for Barkley (even though it's a bad thing for me).

Your former student,
Bastian Fauvell

P.S. I'm going to ask Dad if I can get a new puppy when we get to Hawaii.

P.P.S. It's okay if you let Rachel White read this letter.

Sean

Dear Mr. Fabiano,

When Mr. Peacock found out we been alone all day he jammed us into his office and bawled us out for about fifteen minutes. He said we might get suspended.

But I didn't mind. I was in a double good mood, first because I knew I was going to be walking home with Rachel. And second because Bastian told me he was giving me his puppy!

Me and Rachel walked home without saying anything. Her mom got us homemade cookies and milk and put them on a little coffee table in front of the TV, but I was too excited to eat. I ran almost the whole way over to Bastian's. I was half thinking that Bastian was kidding me, but he wasn't. He cried when he gave me Barkley. And I felt sorry for him.

When Barkley came into the house he ran over to the couch and jumped up on Dad and started licking his face like a lollipop. The puppy likes Dad and Darlene but he's crazy about me. He follows me all over the place. Dad made a little bed for him in the corner of my bedroom but today when I woke up Barkley was sleeping curled up on my bed. And I got a feeling like Christmas morning.

Yours truly,
Sean

Rachel

Dear Mr. Fabiano,

Last night Mom ordered two small pizzas, one with black olives, one with pepperoni. "Which one do you want?" she asked. And it hit me. It probably sounds stupid but when she asked that pizza question a little light went on in my head. I had a choice. Last fall I decided to stop talking. But I didn't have to keep quiet for the rest of my life. I could choose to speak when I was ready. Today it felt like the right time.

I can't wait to tell Mom. And call my father.

I believe we accomplished something important on Friday. Maybe Class 6-238 won't get a place in the *Guinness Book of World Records*. But for almost six hours we were on our own. Jessica thought it was dangerous, and she was 100% right. Of *course* it was dangerous. The first time Amelia Earhart soloed, she nearly crashed. But she survived and so did we. Deep down I believe we did the right thing.

You're going to hear all about me and Bastian fighting during the rock ritual. I still don't completely understand what happened. All I know is, it was the six-month anniversary of Tommy's death, so all day I was thinking of him, and all of a sudden my feelings just bubbled over. I was unfair to Bastian, and I wrote him a note to apologize. Lots of times I wasn't very nice to Tommy, either. I snubbed him the night before he died. I can't change that. But over the weekend I said to myself: "I can live with what I did. I'm not a terrible person." And now I can say it out loud.

Love,
Rachel